PRAISE & ACCOLADES FOR THE
INTERNET GIRLS SERIES

New York Times bestselling series
San Francisco Chronicle bestselling series
Publishers Weekly bestselling series

School Library Journal:
★ Both revealing and innovative, this novel will inspire
teens to pass it to their friends . . . nonnarrative
communication can be a great way to tell a story.

Publishers Weekly:
Myracle's approach is creative . . . an engaging
quick read . . . readers will cheer.

Booklist:
Myracle cleverly manages to build rich characters
and narrative tension without ever taking the story
outside of an IM box.

Kirkus Reviews:
A surprisingly poignant tale of friendship, change,
and growth. Perfectly contemporary. ROTFL.

Teen magazine:
Changing the way you read.

LAUREN MYRACLE

ttfn

AMULET BOOKS · NEW YORK

Cataloging-in-Publication Data has been applied for and may be obtained from the Library of Congress.

ISBN: 978-1-4197-1141-1

Text copyright © 2006, 2014 Lauren Myracle
Book design by Maria T. Middleton

"Chet Baker's Unsung Swan Song" by David Patrick Wilcox. Copyright © 1991 by Irving Music, Midnight Ocean Bonfire Music. All rights administered by Irving Music, Inc. / BMI. Used by permission. All rights reserved.

"Sunrise, Sunset" words by Sheldon Harnick, music by Jerry Bock. Copyright © 1964 (renewed) Mayerling Productions Ltd. (administered by R&H music) and Jerry Bock Enterprises for the United States and Alley Music Corporation, Trio Music Company, and Jerry Bock Enterprises for the world outside of the United States. Used by permission. All rights reserved.

ABRAMS

THE ART OF BOOKS SINCE 1949

115 West 18th Street
New York, NY 10011
www.abramsbooks.com

To all the girlies—and yes! even a few guys!—
who shared their IMs with me or emailed me
about life in general. Yahootie!!!

SnowAngel: hey there, zoe-cakes. r we studs or what? 😊

zoegirl: yahootie!

SnowAngel: i have a total adrenaline buzz going, even tho i am completely and thoroughly exhausted. my muscles r gonna be crazy sore tomorrow.

zoegirl: i hear you. can you imagine how in shape we'd be if we did that every day?

SnowAngel: we could call it the winsome-threesome workout-of-the-century. we cld make an exercise video and rake in oodles of cash.

zoegirl: even my toenails are tired

SnowAngel: *flops onto pretend bed and groans*

SnowAngel: i told chrissy what we did, and she was like, "u ran up the escalator at peachtree center? that super-duper long one?"

zoegirl: okay yes, but the critical point is that we ran up the *down* escalator. you did explain that to her, didn't u?

zoegirl: that's gotta be the longest escalator in the world. seriously, it's as long as a football field.

SnowAngel: i nearly lost it when maddie stopped for a breather and the escalator took her down, down, down. she was all, "noooo! i'm losing ground!"

zoegirl: hee hee

SnowAngel: but in the end we conquered it, cuz we can do ANYTHING, baby.

SnowAngel: it's like in "the cave" by my buds Mumford & Sons. "but i will hold on hope . . . and i'll find strength in pain!"

zoegirl: god, i love Mumford & Sons.

SnowAngel: i know. and that one particular song—it's like therapy every time i listen to it.

zoegirl:	i like the line about wanting to live life as it's meant to be lived.
SnowAngel:	i do too, and how even when things are hard, we just keep going.
SnowAngel:	and do u know HOW we keep going? or at least how *i* keep going?
zoegirl:	how?
SnowAngel:	cuz of u and mads. 😊 😊 😊
zoegirl:	awwwww
SnowAngel:	it's true. true blue, me and u, and don't forget to add maddie 2.
SnowAngel:	do u like my rhyme?
zoegirl:	very impressive
SnowAngel:	wait, there's more! er, let's c . . . since 7th grade they did not part, they stayed connected in their hearts. zoe's the good girl, maddie's wild, and sweet darling angela is meek and mild.
zoegirl:	meek? hahahahaha! mild? hahahahaha!
SnowAngel:	fine, miss brainiac. U find something to rhyme with wild.
zoegirl:	"and sweet goofy angela tends to act like a child"?
SnowAngel:	hey now!
zoegirl:	just teasing. you know i love you.
zoegirl:	i've just got kid-type people on my brain, because guess what? i got the job at Kidding Around!
SnowAngel:	wh-hoo! *happy dance, happy dance*
zoegirl:	there was a message waiting for me when i got home. i'm psyched.
SnowAngel:	ah, what joy, to be wiping noses and chasing toddlers. when do u start?
zoegirl:	um, don't freak, okay?
SnowAngel:	why would i freak? ur not gonna say something to make me freak, r u?
SnowAngel:	wait a minute. don't u DARE tell me u have to start tonight.

zoegirl:	the thing is . . . i do.
SnowAngel:	zoe! noooo!
zoegirl:	saturday night's their busiest night! the director wants me to come in for training.
SnowAngel:	but we were gonna watch "Bridesmaids" again! and eat ugly carrots!
zoegirl:	i know, and i will miss eating my ugly carrot very much. but we can watch "Bridesmaids" tomorrow. that'll be even better, because that way maddie can join us.
SnowAngel:	the point being that she has plans tonight too? yeah, rub it in. u've got yr job and maddie has her cousin's wedding and i have a big old pile of poop. thanks a lot.
zoegirl:	angela, you are such a drama queen. and you don't have a big old pile of 💩. you have a delicious bag of carrots! with hopefully at least one ugly one mixed in for luck!
SnowAngel:	😳
zoegirl:	you're not really mad, are you?
SnowAngel:	of course i'm mad! *flames shoot from ears*
SnowAngel:	only not really, cuz this way i can watch as many episodes of "extreme makeover: home edition" as i want, and i will cry and it will be very emotional, if u would just TRY the show then u would c what i mean.
zoegirl:	umm . . . no
zoegirl:	but you know what's weird? and i mean this in the nicest way ever. last year you would have been totally upset if i'd changed our plans at the last minute. i mean, truly upset, with all kinds of wounded hurt feelings. but this year, you're so much more chill. why is that, do you think?
SnowAngel:	cuz i'm a junior, that's why. *struts around in funky

junior-ness* cuz i can drive, even tho i don't have a car. cuz i choose to live my life the way it's meant to be lived, even tho i will be all alone on a saturday night, and even tho there is seriously something up with my parents, not that they'll admit it.

zoegirl:	there's something up with your parents? explain.
SnowAngel:	it's just this feeling i've been getting.
zoegirl:	like what? and for how long?
SnowAngel:	i dunno, maybe a week?
zoegirl:	a week?! why are you just now telling me???
SnowAngel:	it's like they're hiding something. i can't explain it better than that. i keep thinking that maybe i'm making it up, but then i think that i'm not.
zoegirl:	hmm
zoegirl:	maybe it's a *good* thing they're hiding—like that they're taking you to hawaii
SnowAngel:	i dunno, that somehow doesn't seem very likely.
SnowAngel:	but, whatever. i'm not gonna worry about it, cuz i'm the new and improved Chill Angela. u think they wld name a Barbie after me?
zoegirl:	definitely. for her accessory, she could have a tiny iPhone.
SnowAngel:	no, her accessory would be a tiny picture of u, me, and mads, cuz that's why i'm chill for real. cuz no matter what, i've got u guys giving me my me-ness.
zoegirl:	maddie and i don't give you your you-ness. you give yourself your you-ness.
SnowAngel:	"you-ness." now there's a word for ya.
SnowAngel:	my granddad's name was eunice, btw
zoegirl:	your granddad? don't you mean your grandmom?
SnowAngel:	nope, my granddad. only he spelled it "unus."
zoegirl:	ugh. what were his parents trying to do to him?
SnowAngel:	his full name was unus faye. he went by U.F.
zoegirl:	i am so sorry to hear that.

SnowAngel:	yep
zoegirl:	well, on that note, gtg. wish me luck on my first day, which is really my first night!
SnowAngel:	good luck on yr first day which is really ur first night!
SnowAngel:	ta ta for now!

Sat, Nov 20, 5:16 PM E.S.T.

SnowAngel:	hey, maderoo. getting all dolled up for yr cousin's wedding?
mad maddie:	my dear, the dolling is done. and fyi, i look fab.
mad maddie:	the pops, however, has hit a new low
SnowAngel:	ooo, do tell
mad maddie:	ahem. he bought this self-hair-cutter thing, right? cuz he's such a cheapskate that he didn't wanna fork over 10 bucks at lloyd's barbershop. and of course he decides that today, the day of donovan's wedding, is the perfect day for a trim. so i get home to find dad in the bathroom, hair-cutter aloft, and as i walk to my room, i hear the buzzing begin. bzzzzzzzzzzzzzz.
SnowAngel:	what'd he do, give himself a mohawk?
mad maddie:	if only. so then the buzzing stops, and he goes, "oops." "what happened?" i yell. and he says, "i put on the wrong attachment. huh. guess my hair will be a little shorter than usual."
SnowAngel:	uh oh
mad maddie:	and then for some reason he starts asking if i have a safety pin or a needle or anything pokey. i think he was taking the whole thing apart. but no, i did not have anything pokey, so after a while he puts it back together and the buzzing starts again. and then it shuts off. and he starts LAUGHING.
SnowAngel:	oh crap. what happened?

mad maddie: my idiot father forgot to put ANY attachment back on, which meant that when he started up again, he took off an entire strip of hair down to his scalp. as in, bald. and then once he'd done that, he figured there was nothing to do but complete the scalping.

mad maddie: my father is a cue ball, angela.

SnowAngel: oh no!

SnowAngel: that cracks me up that he would laugh, tho. that's so yr dad.

mad maddie: he was all, "what? it's just hair." the moms is massively annoyed.

SnowAngel: if my dad went bald on the day of a wedding, my mom would jump out a window. or push HIM out a window.

mad maddie: ah, well. we'll go to the reception and drink away our troubles, cuz that's what my family does. shld be a good time.

SnowAngel: that blows my mind that u can drink right there with them.

mad maddie: it's cuz we're irish. it's the law.

SnowAngel: my parents would be like, "you are underage. go sit at the kiddie table." but yours are like, "here, have another beer!"

mad maddie: well, they won't be the ones actually giving me beers. they'll leave that to my crazy aunts and uncles. and it won't be beer, it'll be champagne.

SnowAngel: la di da 🍸

mad maddie: and before long uncle duncan will be ranting about the middle east and aunt teresa will be doing the line dance she learned in 8th grade to michael jackson's "beat it."

mad maddie: i'm telling u, donovan's fiancee has noooooo idea what she's in for.

SnowAngel:	sounds fun
mad maddie:	**it definitely won't be boring**
SnowAngel:	do u wish—even just a little—that u and ian were still going out, so he could go with u?
mad maddie:	**not at all. ian is a fleck and i am a plane, high in the sky. that's how over him i am.**
SnowAngel:	swear?
mad maddie:	**ok, maybe not a plane. maybe just a . . . telephone pole.**
SnowAngel:	meaning what?
mad maddie:	**meaning that maybe i do miss him, but what's the point? if ian had wanted to come to donovan's wedding with me, then he shouldn't have broken up with me.**
SnowAngel:	he didn't break up with u. u broke up with him.
mad maddie:	**but only cuz i knew that he was going to. he called me a ball and chain, if u don't recall.**
SnowAngel:	WHAT?!!
SnowAngel:	he did NOT call u a ball and chain. he made that ONE comment about wanting to hang out with his friends more, and u did your porcupine thing where u bristle up over nothing.
mad maddie:	**there was more to it than that one comment. it was obvious i was cramping his style.**
SnowAngel:	omg. only u wld interpret it like that.
SnowAngel:	it's ok to have feelings, u know. it's even ok to miss ian.
mad maddie:	**thx, Dr. Phil.**
SnowAngel:	he adored you, mads. or rather ADORES you, present tense. he would take you back in a heartbeat.
mad maddie:	**well, that boat's already sailed.**
mad maddie:	**nice of u to say, tho. yr so good to me.**
SnowAngel:	yup, cuz i luv ya

SnowAngel: anyway, who knows? maybe tonight you'll meet someone new. maybe you'll meet your future husband!

mad maddie: or maybe NOT. i'm not looking for a husband, angela—sheesh!

SnowAngel: u never know . . .

SnowAngel: so zoe got that job at Kidding Around, did u hear?

mad maddie: such a dorky name, Kidding Around. it's like, "hiya, buddy, watcha up to?" "not much—just kidding around." with everyone slugging each other on the shoulder.

SnowAngel: cuz it's a childcare place, for when parents don't have a babysitter or whatever. KIDDING around. get it?

mad maddie: der, angela. not getting it was never the problem.

mad maddie: yikes, time to motor. old baldie's calling my name.

SnowAngel: have fun at the wedding! tell donovan congrats for me! OH, and you and zoe are both coming over tomorrow, ok? we're having Sunday Afternoon Movie Madness.

mad maddie: that sounds awesome—only not "Bridesmaids." i know it's supposed to be funny—and it is—but it's oddly depressing too.

SnowAngel: we will take a vote

mad maddie: fine, we'll take a vote

SnowAngel: and my vote counts double since it's my house. 😊 buh-bye!

Sat, Nov 20, 10:32 PM E.S.T.

mad maddie: dude! future hubby alert!

SnowAngel: for real???

mad maddie: no. cute boy, tho. very very cute.

SnowAngel: where r u? is the wedding over?

mad maddie: reception. boy's name = clive.

SnowAngel:	CLIVE?
mad maddie:	**but i call him chive, cuz i is witty. friend of**
	donovan.
SnowAngel:	cool—i wanna hear more! call me!
mad maddie:	**can't. lurking behind dessert table.**
SnowAngel:	yr lurking behind the . . . ?
SnowAngel:	maddie. go somewhere and call me, cuz guess
	what? i think i figged out why my parents are being
	so weird.
mad maddie:	**spill**
SnowAngel:	short version: when i told zoe, she was all, "maybe
	what they're hiding is a GOOD thing, angela," and
	i think maybe she's right. i think they're buying me a
	car!
mad maddie:	**holy shit!**
SnowAngel:	i know!!! they keep talking in these hush-hush quiet
	voices, and then they clam up whenever i come
	in the room. seriously, call me and we can analyze
	every last nuance—it'll be awesome!
mad maddie:	**can't, sorry. it's bunny hop time!**

Sun, Nov 21, 11:01 AM E.S.T.

zoegirl:	maddie! how was the wedding?
mad maddie:	**it was awesome, altho i'm kinda hungover. not**
	terrible, tho.
zoegirl:	more, please
mad maddie:	**it was mainly family, so the ceremony wasn't**
	huge, but with my family that's probably a good
	thing. donovan looked great in his tux, and lisa
	looked drop-dead gorgeous.
zoegirl:	what was her dress like?
mad maddie:	**her dress? i don't know. it was . . . white. NOT**
	froufrou. for lisa it was perfect, especially cuz
	she's so tiny. but, like, naturally tiny. healthy tiny.

zoegirl:	did she seem happy? was she glowing? when i fall in love, it's gonna be with someone who makes me glow.
mad maddie:	ok, excuse me while i barf
zoegirl:	whoa, you really are hungover
mad maddie:	uh, no, i was barfing cuz somehow ur channeling angela with this "glowing" shit. why does everyone have to get all mushy when it comes to love?
zoegirl:	i am *not* channeling angela. you cannot compare me to angela, that is so unfair.
mad maddie:	i don't know if lisa was glowing, but she smiled a lot, and at the reception she gave me a big hug, which surprised me. i used to think she was snobby, but now i'm wondering if she's just shy.
mad maddie:	she's not, like, the coolest girl in the world, but she's the coolest girl for donovan, if that makes sense. i think they're good together.
zoegirl:	well, that's awesome. you can be cynical maddie if you have to be, but i want that someday. i want to fall in love for real.
mad maddie:	u don't consider mr. h for real?
zoegirl:	don't, maddie. i don't even like to joke about that.
mad maddie:	about what? the fact that u almost had an affair with your horny english teacher?
zoegirl:	i am covering my ears now. la la la.
mad maddie:	how about his whole christianity kick, can i joke about that? ya gotta admit, it's great material. it's not very often that a guy uses God to try and lure in the girls.
zoegirl:	please stop
mad maddie:	zo, it happened over a year ago. it's ancient history. when WILL i be allowed to joke about it?

zoegirl:	changing the subject. i talked to angela this morning, and she said you met some guy named after a seasoning. cilantro? paprika?
mad maddie:	ha ha. it's clive. i just call him chive. he goes to northside.
zoegirl:	what grade's he in?
mad maddie:	he's a junior like us. he loves music, which is why he goes to n'side, since they have such a good performing arts department. i told him how i wanna major in music AND advertising and then be the person who makes album art.
mad maddie:	we talked forever—he's got GORGEOUS eyes— and then we kinda ended up getting down and dirty-ish in the corner. the moms totally caught us, which was completely embarrassing.
zoegirl:	oh god
mad maddie:	but she was wasted too, so she didn't care. she got all teary and started saying stuff like, "u and clive! it's meant to be!" and i was like, "mom, no. i love being single." and she goes, "r u telling me ur a slut?"
zoegirl:	nuh uh
mad maddie:	then she calls out to all my aunts and uncles in this really loud voice, "someone bring me another drink—my little girl's a slut!"
zoegirl:	i swear, maddie, your family is so incredibly different from mine. there is no way i would ever have a conversation like that with my mother.
mad maddie:	cuz your family is normal
mad maddie:	she was just joking, tho. she was just being wild.
zoegirl:	was chive around for all that? did he hear your mom call u a slut?
mad maddie:	yeah, and he laughed. that's the cool thing about him.

zoegirl:	huh
mad maddie:	i had FUN, zo. the whole night was fun. i know it's not your style, but i had a blast.
zoegirl:	are you going to see him again?
mad maddie:	who, chive? i hope so, but not in a date-y way if that's what ur asking.
zoegirl:	why not in a date-y way?
mad maddie:	cuz i'm not looking for that. we don't all have to GLOW, zo. we really don't.
mad maddie:	hey, how was your first night at Kidding Around?
zoegirl:	i *love* it. the kids are so cute. there was this one little boy, he was maybe 3, and he had all these fake tattoos on his arm. i would point to one and say, "so what's that?" and he'd say, "a snake, but not a *real* snake." or "a bat, but not a *real* bat." or "a lightning, but not a *real* lightning, because if it was real lightning, there would be thunder. only not here. somewhere else. where the indians are."
mad maddie:	what indians?
zoegirl:	i do not know, to tell you the truth.
zoegirl:	oh—and guess who works there with me?!
mad maddie:	who?
zoegirl:	doug schmidt!
mad maddie:	doug? as in angela's doug?
zoegirl:	he's not really angela's doug, seeing as how she's not the slightest bit interested. but yeah. i was like, "doug! wow!"
mad maddie:	he's gonna be all over u, i can c it now. he's gonna use u as an inside link. angela may not be interested, but it's a sure bet HE is.
zoegirl:	maybe. i just think it's cool that a guy would take a job there in the first place.

mad maddie: what'd angela say?

zoegirl: we didn't talk about it much, because she was kind of distracted. she thinks her parents are buying her a car.

mad maddie: oh yeah, that's right—and she says U planted the idea.

zoegirl: i did not! i just said she shouldn't assume that whatever's going on with her parents is bad.

zoegirl: although i may have to revise that opinion based on a new and not-so-good development. *don't* tell angela.

mad maddie: don't tell angela what?

zoegirl: well . . . i saw her dad at starbucks this morning. i was getting cappuccinos for my parents because i'm such a good daughter, and there was mr. silver. and he wasn't alone.

mad maddie: who was he with?

zoegirl: a woman. a woman wearing a tailored skirt and blouse. the kind of woman who actually uses lip liner.

mad maddie: lip liner, that's hardcore.

mad maddie: so what r u saying?

zoegirl: nothing, i'm not saying anything

mad maddie: u don't think he's having an affair, do u???

zoegirl: no no no, i'm sure he's not.

zoegirl: i just got a weird vibe, that's all.

mad maddie: weird how?

zoegirl: you know how normally mr. silver's so friendly and buddy-buddy? well, today when i went over to say hi, he looked really uncomfortable. all brusque and at the same time blushing, like he'd been caught in the act.

mad maddie: WHAT act?

zoegirl:	i don't know. and he didn't introduce me to lip liner woman, even though she was smiling very pleasantly like "oh, and who's your little friend?" it was one of those moments where he *should* have introduced us, but he didn't.
zoegirl:	there was something suspicious about it. it made me worry that
zoegirl:	never mind
mad maddie:	**what?**
zoegirl:	it's stupid. it's superstitious. but, like, things are going *so well* for us. you're happy, angela's happy, i'm happy. and then i think, crap, when's the bad thing gonna happen, you know?
mad maddie:	**and u think the bad thing has to do with angela's dad and lip liner woman?**
zoegirl:	i didn't say that
mad maddie:	**anywayz, ur crazy. enough bad stuff happened to us last year to last a lifetime.**
zoegirl:	tell me about it. let's see, first there was me and mr. h, then angela and her boy problems, and then as if that wasn't enough, you went all psycho with your wrong and terribly misguided jana obsession.
mad maddie:	**"obsession"? that's a bit of an exaggeration, wldn't u say?**
zoegirl:	no. you were like her clone, mads. you started to talk like her, dress like her . . .
zoegirl:	i am *so* glad you're over that.
mad maddie:	**listen, pal. if i'm not allowed to mention mr. h, then ur not allowed to bring up jana.**
zoegirl:	fine, then you know how i feel.
zoegirl:	but don't you see the pattern? it was last year right around thanksgiving that all that bad stuff

happened, and now here we are, right around thanksgiving again.

mad maddie: **nooooo, zoe. it was BEFORE last thanksgiving that all hell broke loose, cuz over thanksgiving itself, we were blissing out on cumberland island. or have u forgotten?**

zoegirl: of course i haven't forgotten!

zoegirl: why didn't we plan a trip for this year? weren't we going to make it a tradition?

mad maddie: **oops, too late now**

zoegirl: see! that's what's making me feel this way. we're too complacent, just going along like everything's fine.

mad maddie: **yeahhhh, cuz everything IS fine.**

mad maddie: **don't worry, zo. life is good, and ain't nothin gonna change. see ya at angela's!**

Sun, Nov 21, 7:42 PM E.S.T.

SnowAngel: zoe! it's been so long since i saw u—almost a whole hour! u left your sweatshirt at my house, dumb-dumb head. 😊

zoegirl: oops, sorry. would you bring it to me tomorrow?

zoegirl: is maddie still there?

SnowAngel: she just left, *after* patching the butt of her jeans with duct tape cuz she realized they were ripped. it cracks me up, this "i'm such a crazy-ass" stage she's in.

zoegirl: crazy like at donovan's wedding?

zoegirl: it blows my mind that her mom would call her . . . what she called her . . . and she would think it's funny.

SnowAngel: but her mom was drunk. she didn't MEAN it.

zoegirl: yeah, but that makes it even more mind-blowing. do YOU get drunk with YOUR mom?

SnowAngel: hahaha. my mom would be the one marching around and slapping drinks out of people's hands.

zoegirl: i like maddie's mom a lot. and of course i love maddie. i just worry about her sometimes.

SnowAngel: oh, she knows what she's doing, probably.

SnowAngel: what'd u think about chive?

zoegirl: i don't know. i need to meet him before i decide.

SnowAngel: i wish she was still going out with ian.

zoegirl: agreed. ian is such a good guy.

zoegirl: you think they'll ever get back together?

SnowAngel: no, cuz u know how maddie is. when she gets hurt, that's it. there's no looking back. and ian really hurt her, even tho he didn't mean to.

zoegirl: and even though she'll never admit it out loud. she's so funny that way, always having to be so tough.

SnowAngel: like with chive and the whole smooch-and-run incident, u mean?

zoegirl: exactly. i know maddie thinks that's fine—it's her typical maddie no-big-deal approach—but sometimes i think she's putting up a front. i mean, when you fool around with somebody, it has to mean *something* doesn't it?

SnowAngel: u would think so, yeah

zoegirl: she and i talked about that at your house, actually. it was while you were downstairs searching for the dvd. i think i maybe said some things i shouldn't have.

SnowAngel: ooo, like what?

zoegirl: like that i don't agree with the whole friends-with-benefits philosophy. like i think that works out great for guys, but not so much for girls.

SnowAngel: i don't think that's a bad thing to say. why is that a bad thing to say?

zoegirl:	i'm just worried i came off a little harsh. i kept talking and talking, and all these words came out of my mouth, like . . . word-vomit. somehow being with maddie just brings that out in me.
SnowAngel:	word-vomit. lovely. it's pretty hard to offend maddie, tho. i'm sure it was fine.
SnowAngel:	so did u notice my parents and how freaky-deaky they're being? they're thoroughly hiding something. it is so obvious.
zoegirl:	huh
zoegirl:	well, whatever it is, i wouldn't worry about it.
SnowAngel:	???
SnowAngel:	what happened to "i'm sure it's something good" and "maybe they're taking u to hawaii!"
zoegirl:	nothing, it's just
SnowAngel:	just WHAT?
zoegirl:	ok, fine. your dad *did* seem a little off.
SnowAngel:	how so? tell me, tell me, tell me.
zoegirl:	i don't know. he didn't stick around and tease us the way he usually does.
zoegirl:	i guess he just seemed strung out.
SnowAngel:	cuz it is no doubt very exhausting doing price comparisons b/w PT Cruisers and VW bugs. omigod—do u think he's getting me a bug?!!
zoegirl:	er . . . i'm not sure that was the vibe i was picking up.
SnowAngel:	if i got a bug, i could put a daisy in that little flower-holder thing. i think that is so cute, how they come with their own little vases.
SnowAngel:	but a used car would be ok 2. ANY car would be ok. then i wouldn't have to rely on u and maddie all the time.
zoegirl:	i know i said to stay positive, but what if it's not a car?

SnowAngel:	what, now u think it's something bad after all? like that my parents r getting a divorce, or that my dad's got cancer?
zoegirl:	angela, no! i'm sure it's not that!
SnowAngel:	it's not like those thoughts haven't crossed my mind. i overheard my mom talking to my aunt sadie on the phone, and she was saying things like "i'm completely overwhelmed" and "don't know how we'll tell the girls."
zoegirl:	oh crap, angela
zoegirl:	did she mention anything about . . . anything else?
SnowAngel:	anything else like what?
zoegirl:	hold on—just got a text from mads. be right back.
SnowAngel:	zoe!!! u r supposed to be talking to ME, not maddie!
SnowAngel:	get back here this instant!!!!

Sun, Nov 21, 7:59 PM E.S.T.

zoegirl:	angela's all freaked about her parents—she brought it up, not me—and i feel really weird about the whole starbucks encounter. should i tell her about seeing her dad with the lip liner woman?
mad maddie:	shit, don't ask me
zoegirl:	i'm sure it's nothing, but at the same time i don't want to be the one to bring it up.
mad maddie:	then don't
zoegirl:	but if it was *my* dad, i'd want to know.
zoegirl:	i think.
mad maddie:	u think 2 much, zoe. that's your problem.
zoegirl:	you're right, you're right. no need to worry angela over something that could be nothing until we find out for sure!

Sun, Nov 21, 8:04 PM E.S.T.

zoegirl:	hey there, i'm back

SnowAngel:	yr on my bad list *glowers fiercely*
SnowAngel:	abandoning me like that when my father could very well have a deadly disease!
zoegirl:	i'm 99 percent sure your dad doesn't have a deadly disease. really, i am.
SnowAngel:	so what's going on with maddie, who's apparently so much more important than me?
zoegirl:	please. she had a biology question.
SnowAngel:	???
SnowAngel:	u guys aren't in the same class.
zoegirl:	i know, but mr. mack uses the same exact lesson plans. boring boring.
SnowAngel:	oka-a-a-ay, but i'm taking bio too. why didn't she ask ME her question?
zoegirl:	you poor thing! you're having a hard day, aren't you?
SnowAngel:	yes *sniff, sniff*
zoegirl:	oh, angela. you better go have some chocolate, or better yet some ben & jerry's. or both.
SnowAngel:	perhaps i will. in bed with my bunny slippers on and a drop of lavender oil on my pulse points for relaxation.
zoegirl:	👍
SnowAngel:	*takes deep calming breath. takes deep calming breath again*

Sun, Nov 21, 8:10 PM E.S.T.

SnowAngel:	it CLD still be a car. my dad cld be strung out about car payments . . . cldn't he?
zoegirl:	angela, put it out of your mind. you're going to drive yourself crazy. now go get that new york super fudge chunk!
SnowAngel:	ok, ok. good night!

SnowAngel: *stomps into room and plops down on bed*

SnowAngel: am i a happy camper? no, i am not. care to hazard a guess at why?

zoegirl: er . . . did something happen when you got home from school?

SnowAngel: i caught my mom talking to my aunt sadie AGAIN, and in front of her on the coffee table was an empty container of maple pecans, which she only eats when she's stressed. so i confronted her, and she finally admitted that something IS going on.

zoegirl: she did? whoa.

zoegirl: did she say it has to do with . . . life changes?

SnowAngel: life changes?

SnowAngel: omg, do u think my mom's going thru MENOPAUSE?

zoegirl: menopause?! no, i was talking more about . . . life changes in general. when people, u know, change.

zoegirl: but that doesn't matter. just tell me what she said!

SnowAngel: *groans*

SnowAngel: what she SAID is that she didn't wanna talk about it w/o my dad and chrissy. so we're going to dinner tomorrow night, and they'll tell us then. chrissy and i get to pick the place—anywhere we want.

zoegirl: anywhere you want to go? oh no!

SnowAngel: what?

zoegirl: nothing, it's just that it's so Lifetime Movie of the Week. parents *always* let the kids pick the restaurant when they're about to give bad news.

zoegirl: i remember one about a girl whose parents were getting divorced, and her friend was like, "don't pick mcdonald's, because then you'll never wanna go there again. pick some place you really hate." so she picked a chinese restaurant and ended up getting sick all over the table.

SnowAngel:	i'm not picking mcdonald's, and i'm not picking chinese. i'm sorry, but i'm picking some place really good, cuz if they're gonna give us bad news, they're gonna have to do it over a super-nice meal.
zoegirl:	and then there's that strategy, which is equally good.
SnowAngel:	oh god
SnowAngel:	i'm probably not getting a car, am i?
zoegirl:	well . . .
SnowAngel:	i'm gonna call maddie. i have to tell her what's going on.
zoegirl:	chin up, angela. just remember: everyone loves you no matter what!

Tues, Nov 23, 7:31 PM E.S.T.

mad maddie:	hola, zo. ever since i got home from school i've been thinking about angela. u figure she's left for her big family dinner?
zoegirl:	she's probably in the middle of it this very second.
zoegirl:	i'm worried.
mad maddie:	i had the craziest thought about what might be going on. forget the mr. silver's-having-an-affair theory: what if angela's mom is preggers?!!
zoegirl:	what???
mad maddie:	she's not THAT old, u know. she could have some eggs left. and maybe the woman mr. silver was talking to was just a friend, someone he could spill his guts to. and that's why he looked so nervous, cuz he didn't know what u'd overheard.
zoegirl:	oh man, angela would *freak* if her mom's pregnant.
mad maddie:	it would explain all the hush-hush-ness
zoegirl:	you're right, it would

mad maddie:	and i really don't think mr. silver's the type to have an affair, do u?
zoegirl:	i'd be so sad if he was.
mad maddie:	we'll know soon enough, i guess
mad maddie:	in other news, i may be crippled for life. u may have to call me gimpy. or the gimpster.
zoegirl:	huh?
mad maddie:	i was taking a shower and the conditioner was all at the bottom of the bottle, so i turned it upside down and shook it and it flew out of my hand and hit my foot. it totally cut my toe open. blood was, like, swirling down the drain.
zoegirl:	owww!
mad maddie:	"death by conditioner." i can c the obituary now.
zoegirl:	"instead of flowers, the family has requested donations to aveda."
mad maddie:	ha. only i'm a paul mitchell girl.
zoegirl:	paul mitchell doesn't lather
mad maddie:	it does if ur not afraid to slab it on. u gotta be fearless, girl.
mad maddie:	lemme know if u hear anything from angela!

Tues, Nov 23, 8:03 PM E.S.T.

SnowAngel:	call me! now!
zoegirl:	are you at the restaurant?
SnowAngel:	yes. call me!!!

Tues, Nov 23, 8:25 PM E.S.T.

zoegirl:	maddie, you're not going to believe this
mad maddie:	believe what? did u talk to angela?
zoegirl:	just now. she is beyond upset.
zoegirl:	maddie, her dad's not having an affair—he lost his job.
mad maddie:	he what?

zoegirl:	he was fired. isn't that terrible?
mad maddie:	**WHY?**
zoegirl:	i don't know. "downsizing" is what her dad told her.
mad maddie:	**omg**
zoegirl:	and get this: it happened over a month ago. i mean, mrs. silver knew, but not angela and chrissy.
mad maddie:	**he's been hiding it this whole time?**
mad maddie:	**it's so dumb when grown-ups do that. don't they know it always makes things worse?**
zoegirl:	tell me about it.
mad maddie:	**so who was the mystery woman at starbucks?**
zoegirl:	well, i asked angela that—although i didn't mention the affair part, so don't you either. and angela said it was probably his career counselor. he's, like, got to start his life all over again.
mad maddie:	**whoa**
mad maddie:	**what's he gonna do?**
zoegirl:	i don't know. angela couldn't talk long because she had to get back to the table, but she said she'll tell us more when she gets home.
mad maddie:	**man oh man**
zoegirl:	i *told* u something bad was gonna happen. i told you things couldn't go on being so great forever.
mad maddie:	**jesus. i guess u were right!**

Tues, Nov 23, 9:20 PM E.S.T.

SnowAngel:	my life is hell—complete and utter hell!!!!
mad maddie:	**i know, angela. i'm so sorry.**
SnowAngel:	no, u DON'T know. it's so much worse. i can't even talk, cuz i'm crying so hard. i can't even make my thumbs punch in the right letters!
zoegirl:	angela! what's going on? WHAT'S worse?

mad maddie:	CALL ME, YOU BIG DUMMY! call me and i'll add zoe in. then you can tell us instead of bad-thumb-typing us.
SnowAngel:	if i cld talk, i wld. but i can't. all you'd hear is me bawling. plus if i heard your voices i'd break down even more.
zoegirl:	angela? you're kind of scaring me. please tell us what's wrong. please?
SnowAngel:	fine. there's no other way to say it, so i just will.
SnowAngel:	my dad's making us move to california!!!
zoegirl:	*what*?
SnowAngel:	i hate my parents. i hate everyone! why is this happening?!!!
mad maddie:	ur moving to CALIFORNIA???
mad maddie:	NOOOOOO. angela, that's crazy!
zoegirl:	you *can't* move! you . . . you can't!
SnowAngel:	well, apparently i can, cuz i'm a TEENAGER and i have no control over my life! i have to do what my stupid PARENTS say, even if it's the most horrible thing in the entire world!
zoegirl:	wait—slow down
zoegirl:	your dad lost his job, and that majorly majorly sucks. but how did we get from there to california???
SnowAngel:	cuz all this time when my dad's SUPPOSEDLY been at work, he's actually been meeting with his career counselor and filling out online applications. that's how!
mad maddie:	zoe thought your dad was having an affair, btw
SnowAngel:	WHAT???
mad maddie:	she did. she thought the career counselor was his lover.
zoegirl:	maddie!!!
SnowAngel:	i don't care. i wish the career counselor WAS his

	lover, cuz believe me, that would be better than the truth.
SnowAngel:	he applied to this one company in el cerrito, and they offered him a position. they want him to start right away!
zoegirl:	el cerrito? where's el cerrito?
mad maddie:	angela, listen to me. forget el cerrito, forget your dad's career counselor lover. U R NOT ALLOWED TO MOVE.
mad maddie:	your dad hasn't said yes, has he?
SnowAngel:	he hasn't accepted the job YET, but he's flying us out to look at housing. he's trying to make it sound "fun." we're going over thanksgiving!
mad maddie:	THANKSGIVING?!!
zoegirl:	angela, please tell me you're kidding. thanksgiving is this thursday!
SnowAngel:	we're having turkey at my aunt sadie's at 11:00, and then we're catching a 3:30 flight to california. our meal won't even be digested by then! it's insane!!!
zoegirl:	i can't believe they just *sprung* this on you. this is so awful!
SnowAngel:	i know! dad was all, "we didn't want to worry u w/o reason, we wanted to work out the details." and i was like, "were u EVER gonna tell us, or were u just gonna stick us on a plane and be like, `good-bye, old life. hello, el cerrito!'"
SnowAngel:	crap, i can't do this. my hands are shaking. my whole body is shaking.
mad maddie:	want us to come over?
SnowAngel:	will u?
mad maddie:	of course, and we'll figure out how to beat this. we will, angela. CUZ U R NOT MOVING TO CALIFORNIA.

SnowAngel: what about u, zoe? will your mom let u out of the house this late?

zoegirl: i'll lie to her if i have to. i'll tell her i have to go buy new highlighters.

SnowAngel: plz come quick

mad maddie: we're on the way!!!

Wed, Nov 24, 4:30 PM E.S.T.

mad maddie: god, zoe, poor angela. she was like a zombie today, wandering around school with that beat-up expression on her face.

zoegirl: i know. i feel terrible. 😞

mad maddie: yeah, i could tell. every time i saw u, u gave me a death look.

zoegirl: that wasn't because of angela. that's because i'm still mad at you about the whole mr. silver thing. i can't believe you told her i thought her dad was having an affair!

mad maddie: i'm sorry i'm sorry i'm sorry. how many times must i apologize?

mad maddie: but c'mon, angela knew not to take it seriously. she's good that way.

zoegirl: she's good *every* way

zoegirl: i can't live without her, mads. i can't even imagine it.

mad maddie: i can't either. but i thought about it on my way home, and i have an idea. the silvers will fly to california tomorrow, and angela will tell her dad she hates el cerrito, and that'll be the end of it. cuz mr. silver can't say no to angela, right?

zoegirl: i don't know. he's said no to her before. like when she wanted to build a fire pit in their backyard, remember?

mad maddie: just so we could roast marshmallows, which is such an angela kind of thing to wanna do.

zoegirl: and then we roasted them anyway in the oven, and the pot holder caught on fire and mr. silver had a fit. poor angela!

mad maddie: AAARGH, my head hurts. we have to talk about something else or i'm gonna explode.

mad maddie: did i tell u i almost found a googlewhack?

zoegirl: ???

mad maddie: it's distraction therapy. u type 2 words into google. the goal is to get only 1 hit. for example, "toking marsupials."

zoegirl: toking marsupials?

mad maddie: or "phlegmatic weepies" or "crampy dailiness." or my fave, "crapulent porker."

mad maddie: those aren't mine, tho. i can't take credit for them.

zoegirl: huh. pity.

mad maddie: it's extremely hard to find a true googlewhack, but i came close. "flatulent madigan" got 60 hits, while "absorbent madigan" got 636. but "madigan's pantaloons" only got 3.

zoegirl: distraction therapy, you say?

mad maddie: 3, i tell u! this is muy impressive!

zoegirl: i'm not sure i'm grasping the point of all this . . .

mad maddie: the point is that there IS no point. it keeps me from thinking about angela, that's all.

mad maddie: but since U made me think about her again— thanks a lot—do u think she's coming to dylan's party tonight?

zoegirl: i don't know. she's pretty depressed.

mad maddie: which is exactly why she needs to come.

mad maddie: what about u? are u coming?

zoegirl: i have to work first—i picked up a shift since we have tomorrow off. but i'll swing by after.

mad maddie: ooo, you picked up a shift at Kidding Around? nudge-nudge, know what i mean, know what i mean?

zoegirl: maddie? you're trying to make a sex joke about a childcare facility.

mad maddie: it's a stupid name. i can't help it.

mad maddie: so shld i invite chive to dylan's? i wanna invite him to do SOMETHING, only i don't want it to be boring, which i'm fairly sure dylan's won't be. do you follow dylan on twitter?

zoegirl: i did, but it made me want to buy him "hooked on phonics." HIS SPELLING MAKES ME CRINGE! so i muted him.

mad maddie: HA. well, apparently there will be copious amounts of beer.

zoegirl: dylan's an idiot to tweet that. what if his parents see it?

zoegirl: tonnie wyndham's in my english class, and last week she said on facebook how she'd plagiarized her book review. only ms. griffith found out, because ms. griffith surfs the net and types in her students' names.

mad maddie: that girl needs to change her privacy settings.

mad maddie: she doesn't seem to have much interest in privacy—or shld i say boundaries—in the first place, tho. today in health, she asked how many calories r in a tablespoon of sperm.

zoegirl: ewww!

mad maddie: wanna know the answer? 9.

zoegirl: that is revolting. mrs. wayker actually knew?

mad maddie: guess it's not the first time it's come up.

mad maddie: ha—come up, get it?

zoegirl: i am *never* giving anyone a blow job, not even my husband.

mad maddie:	bullshit. u totally will.
zoegirl:	why would you say that? it's disgusting!
mad maddie:	prude, prude, prude. when u find the person who makes u GLOW, u'll go down on him quick as a wink. and then HE'LL glow. you'll blow; he'll glow.
mad maddie:	god, i'm on a roll. this stuff just comes out of me—i don't even have to try.
zoegirl:	maddie, there's nothing here for you to be proud of. hate to break it to you.
mad maddie:	blah blah blah. i'm gonna make the bold move and call chive, and then i'll text angela and tell her that she's required to go too.

Wed, Nov 24, 5:41 PM E.S.T.

mad maddie:	hey, girl. ready for dylan's party?
SnowAngel:	dylan's party? that's tonight?
mad maddie:	yeah, and newsflash: you're coming. and so is chive! wh-hoo! so u'll get to meet him, which u claim u've been wanting to do.
mad maddie:	more importantly, it'll get u out of yr funk. u've been moping about in your room ever since u got home from school, haven't u?
SnowAngel:	yes and no. i was moping for a while, but it wasn't helping, and all i could think about was how terrible everything is. so i rode my bike to little five points to clear my head.
mad maddie:	huh. exercise. not familiar with the concept.
mad maddie:	did it work?
SnowAngel:	well, it's not like i'm leaping up and down for joy, but i don't feel QUITE so suicidal anymore.
SnowAngel:	wanna know why?
mad maddie:	er . . . why?
SnowAngel:	cuz of what happened when i got back home, which i am calling my GREAT BRACELET

BREAKTHROUGH. *strikes a tragically romantic pose* even in these darkest of times, i found a light at the end of the tunnel.

mad maddie: **angela, what the hell r u talking about?**

SnowAngel: i parked my bike when i got to little five points, and i did a little window shopping. and i found a bracelet that i love sooooo much. it's made out of brown leather, and the ends connect with a silver clasp, and on the front there's a slender silver rectangle with the word "believe" etched onto it.

SnowAngel: i know ur gonna say it's corny, but it's like fate was jumping out at me and telling me that everything's gonna be all right. telling me to BELIEVE.

mad maddie: **oh, angela, ur not gonna start carrying around little pewter angels, r u? or those stones that say "joy" or "happiness" or—god help us—"believe"?**

SnowAngel: don't u WANT me to believe?

SnowAngel: why r u making fun of me when i'm actually feeling the tiniest bit better?

mad maddie: **i'm not making fun of U. i'm making fun of those dorky stones.**

SnowAngel: back to my bracelet. in order to look right, it has to be fastened nice and snug, cuz otherwise the "believe" part rotates around where it's not supposed to. i was able to get it PRETTY tight, but not just-right tight, cuz it kept slipping out of place just when i thought i had it.

mad maddie: **why didn't u get chrissy to fasten it for u? or me? u could have brought it to the party and i would have fastened it for u.**

SnowAngel: cuz it became this big thing. cuz in my head i was like, "am i the kind of person who gives up? no. am i the kind of person who fights to the end? yes."

mad maddie: **over a bracelet?**

SnowAngel:	here is what i finally did, and i think i should get a medal cuz it was so brilliant. i hooked one of my necklaces to the end of the bracelet to make the bracelet longer, sort of. and then i used my teeth to pull the necklace tight, which in turn pulled the bracelet tight. then i used my free hand to reach around and fasten the clasp—effortlessly, i tell u!— and voila, my bracelet is on and gorgeous. and every time i look at it, i just think about how things CAN work out if u make them. isn't that good? 😃
mad maddie:	**well, lord love a duck**
SnowAngel:	i know i have to get on that stupid plane tomorrow, but we haven't moved YET. i just have to believe.
mad maddie:	**does this mean u'll come to the party?**
SnowAngel:	can u give me a ride?
mad maddie:	**hells yeah—i'll pick u up in an hour!**

	Wed, Nov 24, 6:30 PM E.S.T.
zoegirl:	hey, angela. i'm texting from work, so i've got to be quick.
SnowAngel:	hey, girl. wassup? ur coming to dylan's, right?
zoegirl:	eventually, just not till after work.
zoegirl:	listen, i just wanted to say . . . well, i'm sorry i thought your dad was having an affair.
SnowAngel:	oh yeahhhhhh. THAT.
zoegirl:	i don't know why i even thought that. pretty stupid, huh?
SnowAngel:	don't worry about it. i told my dad, tho.
zoegirl:	you told your *dad*?
zoegirl:	omigosh. did you tell him it was me who said it?
SnowAngel:	of course. i said it to get back at him for all the crap he's putting me thru, but it backfired cuz he just laughed. my mom thought it was pretty funny too.
zoegirl:	angela!

SnowAngel:	they said to tell u they have a very fulfilling sex life. aren't u glad u brought it up?
zoegirl:	this is so embarrassing! i can't believe you *told* them!!!
SnowAngel:	oh well
SnowAngel:	c ya at dylan's!

Thu, Nov 25, 11:45 AM E.S.T.

mad maddie:	good morning to u on this lovely day of giving thanks, which we americans call thanksgiving, and which wld be far lovelier if not for the taste of sour beer wafting about my tonsils.
mad maddie:	can anyone say cottonmouth?
zoegirl:	hi, mads. i see you're still recovering from last night.
mad maddie:	that was so much fun. i kissed chive on the washing machine, did i tell u?
zoegirl:	yes, maddie. you called me from your cell phone even though i was 20 feet away having a very nice conversation with doug, which you interrupted. you were all, "i'm kissing chive on the washing machine! hahaha, isn't that hilarious? i'm kissing chive on the washing machine!"
mad maddie:	cuz u r my friend. cuz i wanna share my life with u.
zoegirl:	and then you gave your phone to chive and made him talk to me. it was very random and unnecessary.
mad maddie:	i did not make chive talk to u.
mad maddie:	did i?
zoegirl:	you don't remember? afterward, doug and i talked about how much we hate it when people do that. "here, talk to my great-aunt zelda." "here, talk to my buddy from camp whom you've never met and never will."

mad maddie:	**weird. well, what did u say to chive on the phone? what did HE say?**
zoegirl:	he was nice, i guess. he was like, "let's see, you're the shy one, right?"
zoegirl:	maddie, did u tell him i was shy?
mad maddie:	**i dunno, i might have**
zoegirl:	why?
mad maddie:	**what do u mean, why? cuz ur my bud.**
mad maddie:	**i told him all about angela too**
zoegirl:	well, that's sweet, but please don't go around telling people i'm shy.
mad maddie:	**but u R shy**
zoegirl:	a little, maybe. with some people. but it made me feel dumb.
mad maddie:	**chive made u feel dumb?**
zoegirl:	noooo, not chive. he must have realized i was embarrassed, because he said, "hey now, nothing wrong with being shy. just don't be afraid to let loose, okay? you can't always stand around with your hands in your pockets. sometimes you've got to bust a move!"
mad maddie:	**ha. bust a move. not sure how that relates to being shy . . .**
mad maddie:	**so did u like him? don't u think he's awesome?**
zoegirl:	i did like him. he had that drunk-and-sincere thing going on, but he was kind of charming.
mad maddie:	**he's cute too. more like gorgeous.**
zoegirl:	if you say so. but what's going on here? i thought you and chive were just friends.
mad maddie:	**we r!**
mad maddie:	**what, u think i wanna be his girlfriend?**
zoegirl:	doug assumed you were. he saw the two of you together, and he said it looked like you were really into each other.

mad maddie: that's just chive. he does this deep-gaze thing when ur talking to him, as if ur the only person in the whole world that matters.

zoegirl: well, like i said, doug thought you were a couple.

mad maddie: doug, doug, doug. why the obsession with doug? anyway, the two of u hung out for the whole party, but that doesn't make YOU a couple, now does it?

zoegirl: hanging out versus hanging all over . . .

zoegirl: kidding!

mad maddie: i'm gonna let that slide, cuz at least i'm getting some.

zoegirl: ick! maddie!!!

mad maddie: it was cool that doug came to dylan's, though. i don't usually see him at those parties.

zoegirl: we were chatting at work, and i told him about it. i thought it was cool that he came too. i was glad.

mad maddie: i liked his shirt

zoegirl: "tough guys wear pink"? he wore it on purpose for the kids at Kidding Around. graham especially. (graham's that adorable three-year-old i told you about.)

zoegirl: last week graham wore pink socks, and a girl named ashleigh told him that only girls are allowed to wear pink.

mad maddie: alas, it starts so young

zoegirl: but graham didn't seem phased. i call him graham cracker.

mad maddie: bet he's never heard that in all his 3 yrs

zoegirl: last night i played candyland with him, and i let him land on queen frostine even though that wasn't the card he drew. he said, "you're the best, zoe." he kept saying it over and over. "you're the best."

mad maddie: awwww

mad maddie: so i thought angela did pretty well with the whole party thing, didn't u?

zoegirl: freakily well, given all that's going on.

mad maddie: no doubt cuz of THE BRACELET

zoegirl: ah, yes, *the bracelet*

mad maddie: but now she's having her thanksgiving dinner at eleven in the frickin morning and preparing to jet off to california. isn't that just wrong?

zoegirl: i hate that. it makes me so worried for her.

mad maddie: worrying won't do anything. it'll only stress u out.

zoegirl: yeah, but *not* worrying about it is like . . . denial. i mean, there's a very real chance that she'll have to move.

mad maddie: and there's even a realer chance that she won't. stop being a negative nelly.

mad maddie: and now the googlewhack attempt of the day. let's c, how about "graham's hero" . . .

zoegirl: you're changing the subject!

mad maddie: i'm sorry to report that graham's hero got 876,000 hits. guess ur not as special as u thought u were, zo.

zoegirl: maddie, this is what denial *is*! doing everything you can to deny that something's happening!

mad maddie: no, this is called having fun on the computer searching for the perfect 1.

mad maddie: i know, i'll try "sudsy canoodle," in honor of chive.

mad maddie: good lord—4,820 hits. what is wrong with the world?!

zoegirl: um, hate to burst your bubble, but i just tried "inchoate despot" and got only one hit. then I tried "insouciant lavalier" and got ZERO hits!

mad maddie: what? no. impossible. hold on . . .

mad maddie: phew, i am right and you are wrong. *i* just tried "insouciant lavalier" and got 15,200 hits.

zoegirl: but . . .

zoegirl: huh???

mad maddie: zoe, hate to burst *your* bubble, but u can't use quote marks when u google yr two words. u know that, right?

zoegirl: oh.

mad maddie: yes. oh. which reaffirms my point: the world is OUT THERE, and it is wild and woolly and filled with things both possible AND impossible. so until we know which category angela's move falls into—don't worry!!!

Thu, Nov 25, 2:45 PM E.S.T.

SnowAngel: hey, mads. i'm at one of those airport newstands. it sucks. i told my parents i needed gum, but really i needed to get away from them.

mad maddie: hey, girl! sorry about the suck, but i'm so glad to hear from u! when does your plane take off?

SnowAngel: too soon, that's all i know. let's talk about something else. let's talk about the party.

mad maddie: i'm totally with u.

mad maddie: what'd u think of chive?

SnowAngel: oh, he's CUTE, maddie! he's thoroughly cute, in a stoner boy kinda way.

mad maddie: chive is SO not a stoner boy. u just think that cuz he likes to party.

SnowAngel: no, i think that cuz of the way he acts, cuz of the way he looks at u all lazy and slow and appreciative. u know, like, "it's cool, dude." that's his vibe.

mad maddie: that's his VIBE?

SnowAngel: u know who he reminds me of? Matthew McConaughey, with that sexy smile of his.

mad maddie: i'll take that. matthew m. is hot.

mad maddie: and i'm very impressed u can spell his name.

SnowAngel: cuz i read "People"

mad maddie: **but chive is so much more than "it's cool, dude."**
                 he's really into philosophy, and he's taking all
                 these literature classes. did u hear him quoting
                 charles bukowski while dylan funneled a beer?

SnowAngel: who's charles bukowski?

mad maddie: **and that whole story about his dog, napoleon,**
                 and how he's gonna pimp him out by putting
                 a gold chain around his neck. that cracked
                 me up.

SnowAngel: i liked the fact that he went to the keg and got u
                refills. that was very gentlemanly.

mad maddie: **a few too many refills, unfortunately**

SnowAngel: well, i wasn't gonna say anything . . .

mad maddie: **i was so wasted i fell off the toilet seat. it was**
                 hysterical.

SnowAngel: yes, it sounds hysterical *looks extremely suspiciously
                at friend*

mad maddie: **oh, don't go all zoe on me. i didn't tell her about**
                 that little incident, btw.

SnowAngel: fine, but i DO worry about u. just a little.

mad maddie: **u don't need to. sometimes i get kinda psycho,**
                 but it's all fun and games.

mad maddie: **so were u surprised to see doug?**

SnowAngel: that was so awesome that he came! i'm so proud of
                zoe for inviting him.

SnowAngel: and for the record, she looked adorable in her
                embroidered jeans and that soft white shirt that
                actually shows off the fact that she's a girl. i was like,
                "wow, did she dress up for the party?"

mad maddie: **nah, not our zo. sez she came straight from work.**

SnowAngel: with doug. i know. i made a point of talking to him,
                cuz he seemed so shell-shocked at being at a real
                live party.

mad maddie:	oh no, teenagers on the loose! oh no, underage drinking!
SnowAngel:	do u think he seemed different somehow? last night he kinda seemed cuter to me than usual.
mad maddie:	u r so funny. u just think that cuz for the first time in recorded history, he wasn't slobbering all over u. all of a sudden he's unattainable, so u miraculously think he's cute.
SnowAngel:	unattainable? who says he's unattainable?
SnowAngel:	not that i WANT to attain him . . .
mad maddie:	no, u just want him to lust after u in a constant state of angela-worship, like he did all last year. admit it!
SnowAngel:	maybe he's gotten taller. maybe that's what it is.
SnowAngel:	anyway, i kinda ended up flirting with him a bit too much—i don't even know why. but that's ok, i'm sure he'd rather be flirted with than not flirted with.
mad maddie:	a pity flirt. yr too kind.
SnowAngel:	aren't i? i should give lessons to zoe. when i interrupted the two of them, she just stood there like a doormat. i was like, "liven up, zo! ur never gonna catch a guy like that!"
mad maddie:	from where i stood, i'd say zoe was doing just fine.
SnowAngel:	with DOUG? 🙂
SnowAngel:	they're just friends. anyway, u were drunk, so yr judgment doesn't count.
mad maddie:	ugh, don't remind me
SnowAngel:	crudballs, they announced that it's time to board the plane.
mad maddie:	wait, don't go!
SnowAngel:	i have to. i have no choice
mad maddie:	well, call me from california—i want to hear how everything goes.

SnowAngel: i'll try, but my battery's low and i forgot my stupid
                charger.
SnowAngel: real quick—did u like my "believe" bracelet?
mad maddie: i did, oddly enough. i liked it very much.
SnowAngel: i keep touching it and looking down to admire it. i
                know it's stupid, but it gives me strength.
mad maddie: power to the bracelet! all bow down and chant
                "believe"!

                Thu, Nov 25, 7:06 PM E.S.T.
mad maddie: the Kinnick Family Dinner of Thanksgiving
                has mercifully ended, and now i'm at java joe's
                escaping the hellhole that is my house.
zoegirl: why is your house a hellhole?
mad maddie: cuz the moms is on her third glass of chardonnay,
                and the dishes are stacked to the ceiling. my
                brother's girlfriend has taken it upon herself to
                wash them, only she insists on doing it au naturel
                cuz its better for the environment. she sent me
                out for dish soap—that's what i'm supposedly
                doing.
zoegirl: mark's still going strong with pelt-woman, huh?
zoegirl: omg. i just realized something horrible. we've
                been calling her pelt-woman for so long that i
                can't remember her real name!
mad maddie: her armpit hair is long enough to braid, zoe. her
                name IS pelt-woman.
mad maddie: hey, have u talked to angela?
zoegirl: i did, but not for long because her phone died.
                short version: she's not having fun.
mad maddie: well, that's the surprise of the century.
mad maddie: holidays suck. there's so much pressure.
zoegirl: i like holidays
mad maddie: that's cuz ur zoe and u've got the perfect family.

	that's cuz your mom and dad aren't gonna end up throwing beer cans at each other.
zoegirl:	maddie, your parents are not gonna throw beer cans at each other.
zoegirl:	are they?
mad maddie:	fine, wine bottles. and chumley the psycho kitty will attack the remains of the turkey, and before the night is over, pelt-woman will insist that we write something in her gratitude journal. and i will write, "i am grateful that the moms' empty chardonnay bottle only dislocated my shoulder and not my brain."
zoegirl:	you are so full of it
zoegirl:	who's chumley the psycho kitty?
mad maddie:	don't ask
zoegirl:	i just did
mad maddie:	oh. right.
mad maddie:	chumley is mark and pelt-woman's new cat. he's living with us until mark finds a place of his own.
zoegirl:	and when will that be?
mad maddie:	never, cuz he's a loser. he's 22 yrs old and the moms still tucks him in at night.
zoegirl:	lol
mad maddie:	and ppl wonder why i have issues? exhibit a: my family.
zoegirl:	aw, mads, *we're* your real family. me and angela.
mad maddie:	believe me, i'd much rather be giving thanx with u guys. last year at this time, we were all sleeping under the stars on cumberland island. man, that was awesome.
zoegirl:	hold on. *i* was sleeping under the stars, and i froze my booty off. *you* were hogging the tent.

mad maddie:	the stars were pretty, tho. admit it.
mad maddie:	uh oh, there's a goatee boy hovering behind me. he's saying, "um, excuse me, but the sign says tables are 'for paying customers only'?"
zoegirl:	he can't see what you're texting, can he?
mad maddie:	hell if i care. r u, goatee boy? r u reading what i'm writing?
mad maddie:	HA. he's pretending not to, but i can c from over my shoulder that he is. he looks all pinched and constipated.
mad maddie:	alas, i must away to the grocery store. the dish soap is calling my name.
zoegirl:	goatee boy will be so happy
mad maddie:	nah, i'm giving my table to a girl on my other side. she has been waiting very patiently. she gets five gold stars! ⭐ ⭐ ⭐ ⭐ ⭐

Fri, Nov 26, 11:00 AM P.S.T.

SnowAngel:	hiya, zo! hiya, mads! 😊
SnowAngel:	i'm txting from our crudballs hotel. well, at least they let me borrow a phone charger from the front desk. but still. crudballs. you both there?
zoegirl:	angela!!!!! hellooooo!
mad maddie:	maddie kinnick, checking in for duty. angela: how goes it??? did u convince your dad that california sucks?
SnowAngel:	yeah, right. my dad doesn't CARE what i think.
SnowAngel:	guys . . . he took the job! he's starting in december!!!
mad maddie:	WHAT?
SnowAngel:	we're moving to california. we're frickin moving to california!
zoegirl:	omg, angela. in december???
SnowAngel:	dad's leaving in december. the rest of us r staying in atlanta until our house gets sold.

SnowAngel: after that, we're gone!

mad maddie: nooooo, u can't move! u belong here with us!

SnowAngel: u think i don't know that?

SnowAngel: and to add to the suckiness, my dad's boss has an awful daughter WHOM I DETEST. her name's glendy, if that doesn't say enough!

mad maddie: glendy? sounds like a brand of toilet paper.

SnowAngel: she IS a brand of toilet paper. she's horrible.

zoegirl: when did you meet her?

SnowAngel: last night, cuz we ended up having thanksgiving dinner at mr. boss's house instead of the hotel restaurant. aren't i lucky?

SnowAngel: glendy was a freak, all big-eyed and blinky and burble-laffing every time i said anything, which was ridiculous cuz believe me i wasn't being remotely funny. she acts as if she's been homeschooled.

mad maddie: how old is she?

SnowAngel: she's 16 like us—not that u'd guess it cuz she's CLUELESS. she wanted to know where i got my glitter eyeshadow, and i was like, "at the store, u idiot." i was like, "don't u know your dad is an evil selfish pig? don't u know he's stealing my life away?"

zoegirl: oh, poor angela!

SnowAngel: and later she was all, "after u move here, we can have sleepovers! we can give each other beauty treatments!!!" *slits wrists*

mad maddie: so when r u coming back?

SnowAngel: sunday. i can't wait. my mom thinks i'm being a brat cuz i'm not "appreciating this rare chance to c california," but i could care less. 😕

SnowAngel: she's all, "consider this an opportunity," but i don't want an opportunity! i just wanna be with u guys!!!

zoegirl: okay, so you're coming back on sunday . . . and then what?

SnowAngel: the whole fam is flying back to atlanta together, and then dad's gonna pack his stuff and fly out again in a week. mr. boss is gonna find him a place. after that, who knows?

SnowAngel: oh great—chrissy's poking my shoulder and she won't stop. stupid mom told her to tell me to stop texting and get off my butt, cuz it's time to go sightseeing today with mr. boss and glendy. *holds dagger over heart*

mad maddie: shit, angela. i'm so sorry.

zoegirl: me too

SnowAngel: me three!!!

Sat, Nov 27, 10:38 AM E.S.T.

zoegirl: hey, mads. i can't believe it—angela is actually moving! i hoped i'd wake up this morning and realize it was all a big mistake . . . but i didn't.

mad maddie: maybe her dad will change his mind. maybe he'll come to his senses.

zoegirl: i don't think so, maddie.

zoegirl: god, i miss her already, and she's not even officially gone.

mad maddie: zoe, don't

mad maddie: just . . . don't.

zoegirl: i thought maybe you'd wanna talk about it, that's all.

zoegirl: guess i was wrong.

Sun, Nov 28, 4:05 PM E.S.T.

mad maddie: hi, zo. i'm bored.

zoegirl: me too

mad maddie: wanna go meet angela at the airport?

zoegirl: omigosh, what a great idea. she'd be so surprised!

zoegirl: only we can't. you can't go through security unless you're a ticketed passenger.

mad maddie:	**we could wait at the welcome area. wanna? we could bring flowers and candy and a balloon shaped like a unicorn.**
zoegirl:	aw, mads, don't *ever* tell me you're not a big sap at heart.
zoegirl:	but yeah! let's do it!!!

SnowAngel:	k, it's official. my mother is driving me crazy. ever since we got back, she's been in a cleaning frenzy. i caught her trying to throw out a whole bag of old toys, including my complete set of My Pretty Ponies (!!!!), and all she said was, "this house is a junk heap. if i could, i'd throw it ALL away!"
mad maddie:	**even the beautiful Barbie balloon your two bestest buds gave you at the airport?** 🎈
SnowAngel:	well, no, not that. she thought that was very sweet, as did i.
SnowAngel:	but maddie? why did u give me a Barbie balloon?
mad maddie:	**cuz the gift store was out of unicorns. anywayz, zoe said u always wanted a Barbie named after u.**
mad maddie:	**is your mom making u get rid of your Barbies too?**
SnowAngel:	yes. AND my pound puppies.
mad maddie:	**i loved those pound puppies**
SnowAngel:	me 2, except for the 1 with the crusty ear from when chrissy threw up on it.
mad maddie:	**wait a sec, a.**
SnowAngel:	yes?
mad maddie:	**something has just occurred to me, and now i'm a little disturbed. u and zoe and i started hanging out in the 7th grade . . . why were u still playing with Barbies and pound puppies in the 7th grade?**
SnowAngel:	why were U? ur the 1 who just admitted to missing them!

mad maddie:	hmm, ya got me there
mad maddie:	not the Barbies, tho. i could give a rat's ass about Barbie—except when she's big and shiny and made of mylar.
SnowAngel:	aargh. i HATE cleaning. i would actually rather be back at school than at home right now. how sad is that?
mad maddie:	ugh, not me. every single teacher was like, "now that we've returned from thanksgiving vacation, it's time to knuckle down. only two more weeks until final exams!"
SnowAngel:	noooo, i can't handle it! too much pressure! *rips hair from head in clumps*
mad maddie:	u need a glass of nestle quik to calm u down. have u ever noticed with nestle quik how u can actually crunch the chocolatey part? u swish a sip around in your mouth, and the chocolatey crystals just beg to be crunched. it's like at the dentist's, when he says, "ok, now lightly tap your teeth together for me." it's the exact same motion.
SnowAngel:	oh great, my MOTHER is txting me from downstairs. hold on while i see what she wants.
mad maddie:	crunch, crunch, crunch. crunch, crunch, crunch. i'm singing a little song that goes crunch, crunch, crunch.
SnowAngel:	i'm back—sorry about that.
mad maddie:	what'd your mom say?
SnowAngel:	she's such a dweeb. she's like, "hey, sweetie. i know this is stressful, but u've got to remember that it's stressful for all of us. i won't throw away any more of your junk, i promise. love ya, precious!"
mad maddie:	that's so funny that she txts u
SnowAngel:	i know

mad maddie:	it's not a bad idea, tho. hey, maybe i should suggest it to my parents. if they texted me—or better, if they texted each other—maybe they wouldn't yell so much.
SnowAngel:	i don't wanna be here. come rescue me.
mad maddie:	where do u wanna go?
SnowAngel:	i don't care. just come get me!

SnowAngel:	hey, zo-ster. i saw u talking to doug today. r u guys becoming better friends?
zoegirl:	i guess so, yeah
zoegirl:	at work on saturday, this one little girl kept hugging him and telling him she loved him. it was so cute.
SnowAngel:	doug IS pretty lovable, i must admit. sometimes i think, "why in the world don't i just decide to like him?" in some ways it would be so easy—and i know he'd make the perfect boyfriend.
zoegirl:	except i don't think a person just "decides" things like that.
zoegirl:	anyway, there's the small and horrible fact that you're moving to california . . .
SnowAngel:	but maybe if i had a boyfriend, that would make it better. like, he could pine for me and send me flowers. 💐
zoegirl:	*i'll* pine for u, angela. i'll pine for u like crazy!
SnowAngel:	i know, i know. just . . .
zoegirl:	just what?
SnowAngel:	well, u pining for me is good. i thoroughly expect absurd amounts of pining. but do me a favor and don't pine for anyone else, ok?
zoegirl:	huh?
SnowAngel:	doug, i mean. as in u and doug.

zoegirl:	you're telling me not to pine for doug???
zoegirl:	where in the world did *this* come from?
SnowAngel:	omg, it's insane, isn't it? it's just that i saw the way he was looking at u in the hall today, and i got this very weird feeling about it.
zoegirl:	what do u mean, the way he was looking at me? do u think maybe . . . ?
zoegirl:	never mind
SnowAngel:	oh, zoe, forget i said anything. i'm just fragile cuz of everything that's going on with me. it's like, i can't handle any more rejection!
zoegirl:	but angela, you've never been the slightest bit interested in doug. anyway, you had your chance with him last year.
SnowAngel:	but he wasn't as cute back then
zoegirl:	anyway, even if i *did* like doug—not that i do, because like you said that's insane—but in what way would that equal rejection?
SnowAngel:	like i said, forget it
SnowAngel:	i'm gonna go before i say anything else stupid. bye!

Tues, Nov 30, 10:18 PM E.S.T.

SnowAngel:	maddie, a realtor came to our house today.
mad maddie:	**oh god. what'd she say?**
SnowAngel:	that our house is lovely. i hate her.
SnowAngel:	she's gonna send over a "stager" to put in fake plants and stuff, and we're supposed to pop popcorn before any showings so that the house will smell buttery.
mad maddie:	**man, that's nuts**
SnowAngel:	she also said that altho sales are usually slow in the winter, there's a small peak in december. i wanted to stab her eyeballs.

mad maddie: well . . . maybe there won't be a peak in december. try not to think about it.

SnowAngel: maddie, my dad flies out TOMORROW. how am i supposed to not think about it?

SnowAngel: i'm so furious at him, but at the same time i don't want him to leave.

mad maddie: he is a very bad man. i'm furious at him too.

SnowAngel: i'm exhausted. i wanna talk more, but first i wanna lie down. power nap. i'll call you in a while!

Wed, Dec 1, 4:33 PM E.S.T.

SnowAngel: my dad's officially in california. tonight he'll sleep in the new apartment, and tomorrow he'll wake up and drive on new streets to get to his new job.
how wrong is that?

zoegirl: i'm so sorry, angela. i know how you must feel.

SnowAngel: no u don't. u would never be in this situation, cuz your dad's, like, the CEO of his company. he's the one who would be doing the firing, not the one who would ever get fired.

zoegirl: well, he *could* get fired if the stockholders voted him out.

SnowAngel: yeah, fat chance

zoegirl: angela . . . what's going on? do you *want* my dad to get fired?

SnowAngel: aaargh *bonks head on desk*

SnowAngel: no, i don't want your dad to get fired. but i don't wanna move, either. i told mom that i'd rather live in a box outside the mall. i told her i wanna stay here and live with my aunt sadie.

zoegirl: that's a brilliant idea! could you do that—you know, for real?

SnowAngel: mom wouldn't even consider it. she was just, "angela, don't be silly."

zoegirl:	that sucks
SnowAngel:	i know, especially since aunt sadie's the only person in my family who's been the least bit supportive thru all this. i talked to her tonight, and she was like, "don't tell your mom, but i think it's too bad jeff took that job without even considering the other options. a girl shouldn't be uprooted from her friends during her junior year of high school."
zoegirl:	so so so so true
SnowAngel:	yeah
SnowAngel:	that's all i wanted to say, really.

Thu, Dec 2, 7:17 PM E.S.T.

SnowAngel:	maddie, i've got something terrible to confess. i went shopping today cuz i was super depressed, and—er—i seem to have bought a shirt-on-shirt. please don't hate me!
mad maddie:	**huh?**
SnowAngel:	it's sooooo tacky, i know. *ducks for cover*
mad maddie:	**what, pray tell, is a shirt-on-shirt?**
SnowAngel:	it's . . . u know, a long-sleeve shirt with a short-sleeve shirt on top of it, only the long-sleeve shirt is a fake-out, cuz except for the sleeves and collar it doesn't really exist. it's the layered look, so i can look slouchy-cool w/o half-trying.
mad maddie:	**oh, angela, no.**
SnowAngel:	but it's really really cute! the long-sleeve part is white and the short-sleeve part is baby blue to match my eyes.
mad maddie:	**next thing u know, ur gonna be buying fake vintage t-shirts from old navy. ppl will say, "ooo, where'd u get that great shirt? have u really been to bob's hawaiian luau?" and u'll blush and stammer and say, "uh, no, i found it at a thrift**

store," which will be such a lie! UR LIVING A LIE, ANGELA SILVER!!!

SnowAngel: well, it's my aunt sadie's fault. she's the one who whisked me off to the mall. she said i needed some good old-fashioned girl time.

mad maddie: that's nice, altho it's a little unnerving that your aunt sadie considers herself a "girl."

SnowAngel: as opposed to what, a man?

mad maddie: as opposed to a WOMAN. as in, a grown-up adult-acting person our parents' age. not that u'd know it to look at her.

SnowAngel: i know—isn't she adorable? she shops in Gap Kids cuz the jeans there r cheaper, and she's tiny enough that she can get away with it. i wanna be just like her when i grow up.

mad maddie: or when u fail to grow up, as the case may be. lemme guess: your aunt played hooky from work to take u shopping.

mad maddie: did i nail it?

SnowAngel: maybe

mad maddie: and did she have all sorts of funky barrettes jammed in her hair? and was she wearing her hipster shoes with the mile-high platforms?

SnowAngel: so? what would u recommend—turning all matronly and wearing rubber-soled orthopedic loafers? *shudders*

mad maddie: i'm just giving u a hard time. u know i think your aunt sadie is cool.

SnowAngel: we had so much fun at Claire's, trying on all the tacky jewelry. i bought a sparkly dragonfly pin to go with my shirt-on-shirt.

mad maddie: well, aren't u clever

SnowAngel: why, yes i am

SnowAngel: hey, i'm gonna rewatch season one of "orange is

the new black" since it's about prison and since i'm . . . well . . . you know. wanna come watch?

mad maddie: oh, that reminds me. chive posted something funny on his blog. hold on and i'll copy it so u can c . . .

SnowAngel: chive has a blog?

mad maddie: a deadjournal, yeah

SnowAngel: what's a deadjournal?

mad maddie: it's like a livejournal, only better. instead of having "friends," u have "fiends," and your blog's called your grave. the whole site is called the cemetery.

SnowAngel: sounds goth

mad maddie: nah, just antiestablishment

mad maddie: here's his post. it's not about "orange is the new black." it's about reality shows. but it's still funny:

Hey, I know. Let's take a group of twenty-something "actors" and let them pretend to live their lives as if they don't know they're being filmed. Fake-boobed Jersey girl gets punched in face? Check. Famous "model" throws a tantrum in small room crammed with a dozen other famous "models"? Check. "Hunky" bachelor falls in love with not one but TWO lovely ladies? Check.

But so what? It's all in the name of "fun"!

SnowAngel: why is he so obsessed with putting things in "quotes"?

SnowAngel: anyway, how does "chive" know so much about reality shows if he doesn't watch them?

mad maddie: i know, that's what's so funny. chive LOVES reality shows—he just rags on them for the hell of it. in fact he thinks u should move to orange county instead of el cerrito. then you cld be a "TV STAR"!

SnowAngel:	um. okay.
SnowAngel:	i'll run away and live in an alley on hollywood blvd.

⭐

mad maddie:	u, run away? and be separated from your straightening iron?
SnowAngel:	i could stash my straightening iron in my backpack. public bathrooms have electrical outlets, u know.
mad maddie:	no they don't
SnowAngel:	yes they do
mad maddie:	no, angela, they don't. trust me.
SnowAngel:	well . . . then i'd find a library and do my hair there. there are definitely outlets in libraries, cuz ppl use their laptops there.
mad maddie:	i can c it now. to the right are the studious computer folk, working hard on their papers, and to the left is angela, plunked down on the floor and straightening her hair.
SnowAngel:	and the problem is . . . ?
mad maddie:	sorry, darlin, u wouldn't last a minute as a runaway.
SnowAngel:	*sticks out tongue*
SnowAngel:	so r u gonna come watch with me or not?
mad maddie:	i can't—i told chive i'd hang with him. we're gonna watch "doctor who" and down a shot every time someone says "the doctor."
mad maddie:	but tell those prison hotties hi for me!

Fri, Dec 3, 4:15 PM E.S.T.

zoegirl:	hey mads. i'm at my mom's office, sitting in the most phenomenal swivel chair ever invented. can i have a swivel chair like this when i grow up?
mad maddie:	depends. r u gonna be a high-powered lawyer like your mom and make tons of money?
zoegirl:	uh . . .
mad maddie:	i, for one, plan to reject all worldly objects. u can

come visit me in my trailer if you want. i will have christmas lights blinking all year long.

mad maddie: so wazzup?

zoegirl: have you ever heard of

zoegirl: ok, this is embarrassing. i don't know how to say it. which is why i'm txting it.

zoegirl: but have you ever heard of girls, like, pleasuring themselves by jiggling their legs?

mad maddie: WHAT?!!

mad maddie: omg, i am rolling on the floor, just so you know. just exactly how phenomenal IS that swivel chair?

zoegirl: maddie! not *me*! god!

mad maddie: and the term is "masturbating," zoe. u can say it. mas-tur-bat-ing.

zoegirl: fyi, i don't do that. sometimes i wish i could, but i can't, so that's that.

mad maddie: what do u mean, u can't?

zoegirl: i can't, that's all

mad maddie: r u serious?

zoegirl: this is not actually what i texted to talk about. but yes, i'm serious.

zoegirl: can u?

mad maddie: can i MASTURBATE?

mad maddie: uh, zoe, where is your mom? she's not in the room with u, is she?

zoegirl: yes, she's standing right behind me and i'm reading our texts aloud.

zoegirl: she's in a meeting, dummy! i've been stuck at her office *forever* because we're meeting my dad for dinner.

mad maddie: well, in that case . . . yes, i can pleasure myself quite nicely, thank u very much. and i'm only telling u that cuz ur one of my dearest friends on the planet. but don't go asking for lessons.

zoegirl:	oh, gross!
mad maddie:	**what brought this up? what's this "jiggling their legs" business?**
zoegirl:	grrrrrrrrrrr
zoegirl:	chase dickinson, during french. he looked over at me and started cracking up, and i was like, "what? what are you laughing about?"
zoegirl:	he jerked his chin at my legs, which happened to be crossed, and he said, "i know why girls do that."
zoegirl:	"do *what*?" i said.
zoegirl:	and he goes, "jiggle your leg like that."
mad maddie:	**WERE u jiggling your leg?**
zoegirl:	maybe. i don't know. but so what if i was? i wasn't doing . . . what he said i was doing!
mad maddie:	**don't let it bother u. he's an immature freak.**
zoegirl:	i couldn't have been doing that even if i wanted to, not that i *ever* would have been doing it right there in french. i mean, god. but sometimes i think there's something wrong with me, maddie. why doesn't my body work the way other people's do?
mad maddie:	**hmm, cuz ur repressed?**
mad maddie:	**uh oh, ur not responding**
mad maddie:	**i was KIDDING, zoe!**
zoegirl:	that was not a nice thing to say
mad maddie:	**i'm sorry, i'm sorry. i was just teasing.**
zoegirl:	i don't want to be repressed. i just think . . . i don't know. that some girls are more naturally sexual than others. like you.
mad maddie:	**chive told me i'm sexy. he said i have great legs.**
zoegirl:	you do have great legs. you have great everything.
zoegirl:	are you *sure* the two of you aren't becoming an item? angela said you watched "Doctor Who" with him last night.

mad maddie: yeah, and i totally made a fool of myself. not during the show, but after.

zoegirl: uh oh. what happened?

mad maddie: one of chive's friends from northside was there, a girl named whitney, and she was all over chive. it was disgusting. and i guess i was a little . . .

mad maddie: i dunno. but somehow i ended up getting paired off with this guy named brannen, who also goes to n'side.

zoegirl: what do u mean, paired off?

mad maddie: the four of us were out by the pool, which was closed, but we climbed over the fence. whitney was like, "i'll kiss chive, and u kiss brannen, ok?"

zoegirl: she calls him "chive" too?

mad maddie: everybody does now. i love that.

zoegirl: if you're the one who came up with his nickname, and you're the one who likes him, then *you* should get to kiss him.

mad maddie: i know! but whitney already claimed him, so what was i supposed to do?

mad maddie: anywayz, who cares? bodies r bodies r bodies.

zoegirl: no, because bodies are connected to actual people, to hearts and brains and souls.

zoegirl: was brannen cute at least?

mad maddie: ehhh, too short for my taste. and u know what's bad?

zoegirl: what?

mad maddie: it turned into this totally horny go-for-it session, with my bra shoved up and his hands all over me, and now he won't quit txting. he's like, "do u wanna go to a movie? do u wanna go out for coffee?"

mad maddie: i finally wrote back and said, "enough, all right? quit feeling sorry for me."

zoegirl:	i doubt he feels sorry for you, mads.
mad maddie:	that's what HE said. he's all, "what? no, i really like u!"
mad maddie:	whatevs
zoegirl:	i don't get it. you and chive have so much fun together, and it's obvious he thinks you're hot or he wouldn't have kissed you at donovan's wedding. so why would he kiss whitney instead of you?
mad maddie:	cuz she basically told him to. it's not like he was gonna tell her no.
zoegirl:	i don't see why not
mad maddie:	plus she's pretty, in a bouncy cheerleader-y way.
zoegirl:	did he even seem apologetic about it?
mad maddie:	it wasn't a big deal, zo. i refuse to be a ball and chain.
mad maddie:	anywayz, i'm gonna see him later tonight. he says he's got something planned, but he won't tell me what.
zoegirl:	is whitney going to be there?
zoegirl:	this is making me not like chive as much, that he would treat you like this.
mad maddie:	like what? i'm a big girl—i can make my own decisions.
mad maddie:	i can't even blame whitney for liking him. he's just got that kind of energy, where everyone wants to be around him. he makes everyone feel special.
zoegirl:	not special enough, apparently . . .
mad maddie:	i'm so glad u know everything about relationships, zo. i'm so glad ur such a pure and shining example of how to do things right.
zoegirl:	you're right. i'm sorry, i'm sorry.
zoegirl:	and if it makes u feel any better, i have boy problems of my own.

mad maddie: plz elaborate.

zoegirl: all right, but you *can't* tell angela. anyway, it'll probably come to nothing.

mad maddie: what'll come to nothing?

mad maddie: OMG—is it about u and doug?

zoegirl: what?!! how did you know?

mad maddie: it just came to me in a flash, cuz why else would u be all interested in this leg-jiggling business?

zoegirl: maddie!

zoegirl: never mind, i'm not dignifying that with a response.

mad maddie: so you WERE flirting with him at dylan's. i knew it! zoe likes doug! zoe likes doug!

zoegirl: shut up!

mad maddie: omg, if angela finds out she's gonna FREAK.

zoegirl: i know, but why? it's totally unfair for her to even care. yes, he had a crush on her last year, but now they're just friends.

mad maddie: does angela know that?

zoegirl: of course she knows that. she's the one who never reciprocated. how would she think they're anything BUT friends?

mad maddie: cuz in angela's mind, doug is her safety date, the guy who'll long for her forever. and one day she cld have a change of heart, and they would live sappily ever after.

zoegirl: that's not going to happen, maddie

mad maddie: well, no, not with U in the picture

mad maddie: but i'll tell u what: u can't give me a hard time about chive, not when ur sneaking around behind angela's back!

Sat, Dec 4, 11:09 AM E.S.T.

SnowAngel: hi, mads. wake up wake up wake up!

mad maddie:	**ugh. too groggy. go away.**
SnowAngel:	then why'd ya respond to my text, huh? gotcha there, sucker.
mad maddie:	**can't talk. or text, whatever. downloading a song from a group chive told me about. go away.**
SnowAngel:	i'm not going away.
SnowAngel:	so how was your night? *folds hands and waits with a pleasant smile*
mad maddie:	**u really wanna know?**
SnowAngel:	yes, i really wanna know.
mad maddie:	**well, u can't flip out, but i'll tell u cuz ur my friend.**
SnowAngel:	hmm, intrigue. i luv it.
mad maddie:	**i smoked pot for the first time, ok?**
SnowAngel:	WHAT???
mad maddie:	**it was SO not a big deal. chive said he had a surprise for me, and that's what it was.**
SnowAngel:	chive's surprise was that the 2 of u were gonna smoke pot?!
mad maddie:	**and his friend brannen, which was a mistake. not the fact that i smoked pot, but the fact that brannen was there too.**
SnowAngel:	brannen from the kissy-kissy night?
mad maddie:	**if i'd known he was gonna be there, i might not have gone. cuz the pot, like, intensified everything, and partly that was cool, but partly it was uncool, especially in regards to brannen.**
SnowAngel:	why?
mad maddie:	**i dunno, cuz he kept staring at me with this "i'm interested in u" smile. it was gross.**
SnowAngel:	what about chive?
mad maddie:	**he was in his own world listening to music with earbuds in. i wish i could be more like that, just do whatever i feel like doing and be confident in**

	myself. but no. i had to deal with brannen making pop-eyes at me.
SnowAngel:	where were u guys this whole time?
mad maddie:	we sneaked into a housing development called cross creek condominiums. there's this big stretch of forest behind the condos, and that's where we went.
SnowAngel:	oh
mad maddie:	we called ourselves the cross creek crusaders. it was pretty funny.
SnowAngel:	i can't believe u smoked pot. i mean, i know ppl do, but i can't believe that U did.
SnowAngel:	what was it like?
mad maddie:	kinda a mixed bag
mad maddie:	ha, that's funny. a mixed BAG, get it?
SnowAngel:	no
mad maddie:	as in, a bag of pot. that's what u call it.
SnowAngel:	fascinating, now tell me what it was like
mad maddie:	well, it hurt sucking it in. and then ur supposed to hold it for as long as u can, but i kept coughing. and it made my eyes water.
SnowAngel:	sounds fun. NOT!
mad maddie:	chive says i'll get better with practice. he says the paranoid feelings will go away too.
SnowAngel:	huh
SnowAngel:	um, i know this'll sound kinda stupid, but what's the GOOD part about smoking pot? besides the fact that it was something u did with chive.
mad maddie:	well . . . i seriously had some wild sensations. it made everything blurry around the edges, like the boundaries of the world were melting away, and all these undercurrents of life were swirling around us. and i could SEE them. that's what made it so cool.

SnowAngel: u could see what? the undercurrents of life?

mad maddie: i know it sounds weird. i guess there's no way to explain it unless u've tried it yourself.

SnowAngel: my life is blurry enough, thx

SnowAngel: u gonna do it again?

mad maddie: dunno. wish it didn't burn so much.

mad maddie: but chive mentioned something about hooking up tonight, so maybe. wanna come?

SnowAngel: er . . . doesn't really sound like my scene.

mad maddie: yr always saying u want to get to know chive better, and zoe's working tonight so u have no excuse. u don't have to smoke if u don't want to.

SnowAngel: i don't wanna sneak into that golf course, either

mad maddie: it's not a golf course! it's just the woods behind some condos.

mad maddie: how about this: why don't i call chive and see what's up, and then i'll give u more details. we'll do something legal if that's what u want.

SnowAngel: uh . . . ok, i guess

mad maddie: hey, that just gave me a good idea for a googlewhack.

SnowAngel: qu'est-ce que c'est un googlewhack?

mad maddie: i haven't told u about googlewhacks?

mad maddie: oh yeah, that was zoe i told

SnowAngel: *taps foot on floor*

mad maddie: a googlewhack is an extremely delightful way to pass the time where u type in words on google and try to get only one hit. the "perfect 1," it's called.

SnowAngel: sounds boring

SnowAngel: or rather, sounds like something u should do ON YOUR OWN and not while your friend is twiddling away her toes.

mad maddie: i'm gonna try "legal chive," whaddaya think? let me just do a little multitasking here . . .

mad maddie: tarnation. 20,100 hits.

SnowAngel: oh well 🙂

mad maddie: maybe "illegal chive" is the way to go, eh?

SnowAngel: maddie, i do not wanna sit here while u googlewhack!

mad maddie: 716 hits. still shabby. wouldn't it be funny if all 716 were actually about chive and his illegal activities?

SnowAngel: wouldn't it be even funnier if u actually talked to ME instead of googlewhacking off in the corner?

mad maddie: ooo, u make me sound so perverted

SnowAngel: good-bye, i'm leaving

mad maddie: what? WHY?

SnowAngel: cuz ur making my eyes glaze over. anyway, i've gotta clean up my room for an open house today. UGH.

mad maddie: in that case maybe i'll go hunt down some breakfast—maybe some more of that pizza i had last night. u know, pizza hut pizza is truly amazing. it's been in our fridge for 2 weeks, but it tastes as good as ever.

SnowAngel: did u say two weeks? *goes pale*

mad maddie: i didn't even heat it up. mmm-mmm good!
🍕 🍕 🍕

Sat, Dec 4, 11:52 AM E.S.T.

SnowAngel: omg, i just realized! chive IS a stoner!!!

mad maddie: huh?

SnowAngel: i said he was a stoner at dylan's party, and u were like, "nooooo." but he's TOTALLY a stoner boy.

SnowAngel: u knew it all along, didn't u?

mad maddie: well . . .

mad maddie: he's more than that, tho. he's not JUST a stoner boy.

SnowAngel:	i'm just saying. *looks knowingly at friend*
SnowAngel:	u can't pull 1 over on me, madderoo!

Sun, Dec 5, 9:18 AM E.S.T.

SnowAngel:	mornin', sunshine. did u have fun at work last night?
SnowAngel:	zoe?
SnowAngel:	wow, it must have been REALLY good if you can't even take the time to text back yr dearest friend. either that or really bad . . .
zoegirl:	sorry, sorry, texting someone else
SnowAngel:	who?
zoegirl:	just someone
SnowAngel:	okay. WHO?
zoegirl:	it was doug, that's all. he texted me, i didn't text him.
SnowAngel:	doug texted u? why?
SnowAngel:	did he ask about me?
zoegirl:	you know, angela, it's not *always* about you.
zoegirl:	we were talking about work, that's all. about that little kid who cracks us up, graham cracker. last night graham kept presenting his cheek to me and saying, "you can kiss me if you want. little boys need lots of kisses."
SnowAngel:	aww, i love little kids. they're so pure. 😇
SnowAngel:	wanna know what i did last night? and just to give u a hint, "pure" would not be the way to describe it.
zoegirl:	that's right, you went out with maddie and chive! how'd it go?
SnowAngel:	AND meade AND brannen AND whitney.
SnowAngel:	i have to tell u, zoe, i'm feeling weird about it.
zoegirl:	how come?
SnowAngel:	i dunno. i've been trying to figure it out. i've been trying to figure out chive, mainly. maddie really likes him, u know.

zoegirl:	do you not?
SnowAngel:	no, i DO like him—at least when i'm around him. he's smart, even tho he talks so s-l-o-w-l-y. and he's funny. he was totally cracking me up last night, calling everyone "boogie." as in, "m-boogie, what's happening?" or "c'mon over here, a-boogie, and get yo-self some chips."
zoegirl:	he is pretty charming, isn't he? i remember that from dylan's party.
SnowAngel:	AND he's extremely hot
SnowAngel:	i can see why maddie's into him. i just think he holds too much power over her.
zoegirl:	like jana last year?
SnowAngel:	maybe . . . but different. chive isn't trying to use maddie, i don't think. and he DOES care about her, i can tell. he just doesn't care about her ENOUGH.
zoegirl:	maybe he doesn't care about anyone enough.
zoegirl:	you know he kissed whitney, right? but maddie was all, "it's no big deal, bodies are bodies, blah blah blah."
SnowAngel:	last night chive was giving maddie all kinds of attention—laughing at her jokes, looking at her in that lazy, bemused way of his—but he was sitting next to whitney and stroking her forearm the whole time.
zoegirl:	ick. *so* uncool.
SnowAngel:	i'm sure maddie can't be too thrilled about that, but of course she won't admit it.
zoegirl:	i don't get it. there's no way i could watch the guy i like fool around with another girl.
SnowAngel:	"the guy u like"? who's the guy u like?
zoegirl:	what? nobody!
SnowAngel:	then why would u say that?
zoegirl:	why would i say what?

SnowAngel:	zoe, r u hiding something?
zoegirl:	angela, please. we're talking about chive, remember?
SnowAngel:	oh yeah
SnowAngel:	u know he's a stoner, right? well, guess what: now maddie's becoming one too.
zoegirl:	becoming a *stoner*?
zoegirl:	no way
SnowAngel:	she's tried it, tho. she really has.
zoegirl:	hold on. maddie tried *pot*?
SnowAngel:	yes, pot. 🍁 weed, ganja, doobage, gank.
zoegirl:	gank? gank is an extremely stupid word.
zoegirl:	and no, i didn't know she tried it, because of course she didn't tell me.
SnowAngel:	cuz she thinks ur a nun 😊
zoegirl:	that is so irritating. and she shouldn't be smoking pot. it kills brain cells. doesn't she know that?
SnowAngel:	i'm not even sure she liked it that much, from what she said.
zoegirl:	but i bet she pretends she does in front of chive. am i right? to protect her tough-girl image?
SnowAngel:	well . . . possibly. i was afraid they were gonna light up last night, but they didn't. brannen was like, "we're out of pot, dude. who's gonna go on a pot run?" but nobody ever did anything about it.
zoegirl:	lovely
SnowAngel:	crap, i g2g. my mom's yelling at me from downstairs—some family is here for a 2nd showing of the house.
zoegirl:	a 2nd showing? oh no!
SnowAngel:	don't worry, i have a plan. i heard the evil realtor say that the man wants to know about our neighbors, cuz his current neighbors r really loud. so as i leave, i'm gonna happen to mention the

thoroughly bitchin garage band that practices two
doors down. *snickers*

zoegirl:	what garage band?
SnowAngel:	exactly
SnowAngel:	ttfn!

Mon, Dec 6, 10:15 AM E.S.T.

mad maddie:	z-boogie! i saw u hanging out with doug at his locker, and unless i am mistaken (which i sincerely hope i am), i heard him saying something very disturbing.
zoegirl:	what are you talking about?
mad maddie:	ahem. and i quote, "u can kiss me if you want. little boys need lots of kisses." !!!
zoegirl:	oh gosh. you heard that?
mad maddie:	what kind of twisted games r u playing, zo? PLEASE tell me u don't pretend to be his mommy. PLEASE tell me u don't spank his iddle-widdle bottom.
zoegirl:	maddie, gross!!!
mad maddie:	WELL?
zoegirl:	it's an inside joke, from saturday night when we worked together. he wasn't being himself. he was just being . . . cute.
mad maddie:	"little boys need lots of kisses"?!!!
zoegirl:	please stop. you're making me blush.
mad maddie:	have u told angela yet? cuz i gotta say, if ur gonna be flirting with him in the hall, she's gonna find out.
zoegirl:	i know, i know . . . but there's so much going on with her right now. i don't want to make things more complicated. and i don't want to make her mad at me.
mad maddie:	ha—i would love it if she got mad at u. she NEVER gets mad at u.

zoegirl:	maddie, that's a terrible thing to say! why would you even say that?
mad maddie:	that's why u have to TELL her, u idiot. on every single sitcom in the world, this is how problems start. some idiot plays dumb and doesn't tell someone else what's really going on, and then there's mass confusion and mistaken assumptions and everything ends in chaos. u shld know this, zoe.
zoegirl:	i *do* know. i do. but when you're in the middle of it—in real life, not tv—it's completely different. it's harder than you think to tell the truth.
mad maddie:	not for me
zoegirl:	then you tell her!
mad maddie:	no ma'am, miss zoe. i'm having too much fun watching you squirm.
mad maddie:	but i do want u to swear to me that u'll straighten this whole mess out, mmmkay?
zoegirl:	fine. i will. i really will.
mad maddie:	when?
zoegirl:	tomorrow, i promise
mad maddie:	i'm doing this for your own good!

Tues, Dec 7, 9:09 AM E.S.T.

mad maddie:	dude! i know yr in class, but i'm bored!
zoegirl:	maddie, go away
mad maddie:	if you want me to go away, why'd you respond?
zoegirl:	because my phone's on vibrate. otherwise i wouldn't have.
mad maddie:	ooo, vibrate. is it as good as your special chair?
zoegirl:	😠
mad maddie:	have u told angela about doug?
zoegirl:	not yet
mad maddie:	u better!

mad maddie: **how about now? have u told her by now?**

zoegirl: stop texting me during class!

mad maddie: **so u haven't?**

zoegirl: ms. aiken is staring. i'm turning you off.

mad maddie: **hi, zo. me again. do u feel like ur being spied on?**

zoegirl: maddie, what are you doing here? this isn't your free.

mad maddie: **peaches doesn't care. she loves me. anywayz, the media center isn't your own private idaho.**

mad maddie: **have u told angela?**

zoegirl: no, because i'm being stalked by a deranged lunatic who thinks it's more fun to text and make waggly eyebrows than to JUST COME OVER AND TALK TO ME.

mad maddie: **okey-doke, i'll come over and talk to you. in a nice loud voice that everyone can hear.**

zoegirl: on second thought, don't. i'll tell angela as soon as i get home from school. are you satisfied? now go away. i have to finish this paper!

mad maddie: ***singsong voice* yr home from school! HAVE U TOLD HER?**

zoegirl: you're a freak. i'm calling her right now. bye!

zoegirl: hi, maddie. it's me.

mad maddie: **oh really? u mean someone didn't steal yr phone? awesome!**

zoegirl: shut up, smarty-pants.

zoegirl:	i just wanted to tell you that i called angela, just like i said i would, but i didn't tell her about doug.
mad maddie:	**omg. what's your excuse this time?**
zoegirl:	they sold the house, mads. her mom sold the house.
mad maddie:	**WHAT?!!!**
zoegirl:	they're moving as soon as finals are over!!!
mad maddie:	**as soon as**
mad maddie:	**zoe, that's less than 2 weeks!**
zoegirl:	i know
mad maddie:	**i just**
mad maddie:	**i don't even**
mad maddie:	**they're seriously moving? this is real?**
zoegirl:	angela could barely get the words out, she was crying so hard.
mad maddie:	**holy fucking shit**
mad maddie:	**where r they gonna LIVE?**
zoegirl:	the apartment mr. silver rented has three bedrooms, so they'll join him there. i guess that was the plan all along.
zoegirl:	what are we gonna do, maddie?
mad maddie:	**i have no flipping idea**
mad maddie:	**but for now, we better get going.**
zoegirl:	where, to angela's?
mad maddie:	**where else?!**

	Thu, Dec 9, 9:14 PM E.S.T.
zoegirl:	hey, mads. did you read angela's FB status? it's so sad.
mad maddie:	**i know. i was gonna txt her, but all those scowly faces made me think, "ooo, better back off."**
zoegirl:	i had the same thought, but then i realized that right now is when she needs us the most. so i called her—and she sounded *very* depressed.

mad maddie:	well, duh. she's moving 3,000 miles away.
zoegirl:	it was like she wasn't even angela anymore. her voice was all pale and listless, and she kept saying, "this sucks. this just totally sucks."
mad maddie:	that's how she was at lunch too
zoegirl:	i tried in my nicest way to suggest that being depressed isn't gonna help anything, and she goes, "i think it's an appropriate response, zoe." like i was being stupid for trying to cheer her up.
mad maddie:	we shld do something fun tomorrow night. maybe that would help.
zoegirl:	yeah, sounds good. i feel bad that i can't do something with her tomorrow night *and* saturday night, but i've got to work.
mad maddie:	where u'll c doug, nudge-nudge, wink-wink 😊
mad maddie:	u still haven't told angela, have u?
zoegirl:	it's so not the point right now. it would just make her feel worse.
mad maddie:	ur playing with fire, zoe. mark my words, this is gonna come back and bite u on the ass!

Fri, Dec 10, 4:44 PM E.S.T.

mad maddie:	hey, gal. since u never decided what u wanna do tonight, zoe and i decided for u. put your party hat on . . . cuz we're going BOWLING!!!
SnowAngel:	*lifts head from the depths of hell* bowling?
mad maddie:	chop-chop! if we get there early, we can beat the rush.
SnowAngel:	there's a rush to go bowling?
mad maddie:	on a friday night? we're talking high drama, baby. ker-ash! she scores another strike!
SnowAngel:	i haven't gone bowling since last year when i went with doug and steve and chrissy. doug and steve slipped notes into the holes in chrissy's ball

and pretended they were from a mystery admirer, remember?

SnowAngel: that was so fun. but nothing will ever be fun again.

mad maddie: **YES IT WILL. oh, and be sure to wear crappy shoes. don't ask—just do it.**

SnowAngel: pardon me, but i don't own any crappy shoes

SnowAngel: hey, do u think doug would come with us if we called him? maybe that's what i need to perk me up, a dose of doug-love.

mad maddie: **er . . . no doug. this is a girls' night, full of bonding and wacky hijinks.**

SnowAngel: right, right

SnowAngel: but i have been thinking . . . maybe, before i leave, i'll give doug something to remember me by. *wink, wink* he's certainly waited for it long enough.

mad maddie: **angela, no**

SnowAngel: why? it would be the thrill of his life.

mad maddie: **bad idea. trust me.**

SnowAngel: yeah, i guess it wouldn't be fair. *sigh*

mad maddie: **that's right. leave the poor guy alone.**

SnowAngel: altho who said love was fair? and long-distance relationships CAN work, u know . . .

mad maddie: **FORGET ABOUT DOUG**

mad maddie: **now go dig thru your closet and find your rattiest sneaks. i'm coming to pick u up!**

Sat, Dec 11, 10:00 AM E.S.T.

SnowAngel: morning, zo

zoegirl: morning, angela. are you wearing your super-duper very own pair of official bowling shoes?

SnowAngel: at ten in the morning? i'm in my bunny slippers, sweetheart.

SnowAngel:	but yeah, i've got them right here beside me. *pats hideous bowling shoes lovingly* i didn't think we were gonna have fun . . . but we did, didn't we?
zoegirl:	especially when you threw your ball into that truck driver's lane. (snicker, snicker)
SnowAngel:	he could have been MUCH more understanding. it's not like i meant to.
zoegirl:	and then you knocked over his beer when you went to reclaim it, ya big klutz.
zoegirl:	poor guy!
SnowAngel:	poor me! i'm under a lot of stress, zoe. i'm leaving in 6 days!!!
zoegirl:	what i don't get is why you just didn't tell the truck driver guy that you spilled his beer, instead of leaving it glopped on the floor in a puddle. if you'd cleaned it up right then, nothing else would have happened.
SnowAngel:	i didn't tell him cuz i didn't want him yelling at me again. duh!
zoegirl:	and that strategy sure worked
SnowAngel:	it's not MY fault. who knew beer was so sticky?
zoegirl:	and who knew our truck driver friend would attempt his patented foot-slide approach right after stepping smack into it?
SnowAngel:	i think he needs to alter his diet. a slimmer man wouldn't have fallen so hard.
zoegirl:	too many cheese fries
SnowAngel:	at least it caused a distraction as we stole our shoes. frankly, zo, i'm still surprised you went along with it.
zoegirl:	the operative word is "trade," angela. we gave them a more than fair trade.
SnowAngel:	in your case, maybe. i gave them a pair of chrissy's old tap shoes from when she used to take lessons.

zoegirl:	um, angela? why did u just insert a pirate smiley?
SnowAngel:	i dunno. cuz it's cute?
zoegirl:	you're such a goof
zoegirl:	so what are you doing for the rest of the day?
SnowAngel:	i'm PACKING. how's that for a mood kill?
zoegirl:	oh, angela
SnowAngel:	come keep me company, please-please-pleasy-please?
zoegirl:	sure, only i have to go to work at 5:00. and at some point, i should probably study for finals.
SnowAngel:	finals. *vomit*
SnowAngel:	there is no way i can be expected to study when my whole life is being ripped apart.
zoegirl:	maybe we can study together after i help u pack.
SnowAngel:	just come over. i don't care what we do, as long as i'm not alone!

Sun, Dec 12, 3:30 PM E.S.T.

mad maddie:	hey, a-boogie
SnowAngel:	hey, m-boogie
SnowAngel:	how long r u gonna stay on this "boogie" kick?
mad maddie:	for-boogie-ever. got a problem wid dat?
SnowAngel:	ur a freak
SnowAngel:	so wazzup?
mad maddie:	nothing, just procrastinating. i SHLD be studying, but let's just say i'm not.
mad maddie:	wanna go get krispy kremes?
SnowAngel:	heck yeah!
mad maddie:	boogie-licious!

Mon, Dec 13, 5:23 PM E.S.T.

zoegirl:	hey, angela. guess what happened in biology today?
SnowAngel:	what?
zoegirl:	mr. mack tripped on the smart-board cable, and

	he went down hard. he hit his head on his desk and ended up with a gash from his eyebrow to his hairline. blood. everywhere. it was crazy.
SnowAngel:	poor mr. mack!
zoegirl:	he's okay. head wounds bleed a lot even when they're pretty minor, he said. but for the rest of the period (after taping a paper towel bandage to his head with masking tape), he pretended to have amnesia. every time someone asked a question about our exam, he'd be like, "what's your name again?"
SnowAngel:	that's gonna be me at my stupid new school. i won't know a single person's name except stupid glendy.
SnowAngel:	i wish I'D get clonked on my head—at least then i'd be put out of my misery.
zoegirl:	angela!
zoegirl:	i told you about mr. mack to cheer you up, not make you more depressed!
SnowAngel:	oh
SnowAngel:	well . . . ha
zoegirl:	that wasn't very convincing
SnowAngel:	HAHAHAHAHA
SnowAngel:	was that better?
zoegirl:	er, thanks for trying
SnowAngel:	yeah, u too

Tues, Dec 14, 4:09 PM E.S.T.

zoegirl:	i can't believe finals start tomorrow—help!
SnowAngel:	which means only 3 more days until . . . never mind.
zoegirl:	i know
zoegirl:	that's all i can think about, even though i've *got* to focus on studying.

SnowAngel:	there's no way i'm getting any studying done. i've just accepted it.
SnowAngel:	sorry i'm typing so slow, btw. i cut my thumb on the packing tape dispenser, and the band-aid's making things tricky.
zoegirl:	that's okay
SnowAngel:	ms. higgins gave us the question for our take-home essay. wanna hear it?
zoegirl:	sure
SnowAngel:	it's awful. it's like she WANTS to torture me, as if that was her evil plan. "using any three works of literature from this semester, discuss the following quote: 'home is where the heart is.' support your position with examples."
zoegirl:	oh man
SnowAngel:	i know
SnowAngel:	hey zo . . . do u ever just feel sad for no reason?
zoegirl:	i do, yeah.
SnowAngel:	me too
SnowAngel:	*sigh*
SnowAngel:	guess my bracelet didn't work, huh?
zoegirl:	what bracelet?
zoegirl:	oh, your "believe" bracelet
SnowAngel:	i kept thinking that maybe this was all a joke, that maybe it would all go away. i've been closing my eyes and rubbing the "believe" part, as if my wish might actually come true. isn't that stupid?
zoegirl:	not stupid at all. i wish it *would* come true.
SnowAngel:	oh well
zoegirl:	i don't want u to move, angela.
SnowAngel:	me neither 😢

Wed, Dec 15, 6:59 PM E.S.T.

zoegirl:	three finals down, two to go!

SnowAngel:	😶
zoegirl:	i hear you. it's like, yay that we're over half done, but the pressure's still on.
zoegirl:	i've been mowing my way through my mongo bag of snack-size snickers, which i convinced my mom i have to have in order to study. i don't know how it started, but now every year at exam time she stocks up on snickers and coke.
SnowAngel:	while my mom, on the other hand, asks questions like, "have u cleaned out your closet yet? the moving truck will be here tomorrow afternoon, u know."
zoegirl:	do you have to be there for that? because maddie and i want to take you out, since it's your . . . you know.
SnowAngel:	since it's my last night in atlanta?
zoegirl:	yeah. we want to spend every minute we can with you.
SnowAngel:	at least someone does.
SnowAngel:	other than you two, do you know that hardly ANYONE has acted the slightest bit devastated that i'm moving? they act sad for like a second, and then they're all, "omg, have u finished your take-home yet? have u memorized the formulas for chemistry?"
zoegirl:	people just don't know how to handle it, angela. everyone hates it that you're leaving.
SnowAngel:	it's like when u get a haircut and u go to school all self-conscious and waiting for ppl to comment on it, and then no one notices at all. that's what it's gonna be like when i'm gone.
zoegirl:	not for us, angela
zoegirl:	you will leave a hole the size of france.

SnowAngel: me again. my mom says it's fine if i go out with u guys tomorrow night. she said she already assumed that's what i'd be doing.

zoegirl: good!

SnowAngel: i can stay out as late as i want, which i guess is nice of her.

SnowAngel: but it's not enough.

zoegirl: no, it's not.

SnowAngel: ☹

mad maddie: we're done!

zoegirl: yay!!!

mad maddie: do u have the candles & food & quilt?

zoegirl: i do. do you have the pictures?

mad maddie: yes ma'am, in my backpack.

zoegirl: she's going to cry, you know. we all are.

mad maddie: NO WE'RE NOT. c ya at collier park!

mad maddie: woot! woot!

SnowAngel: oh god, i JUST turned my paper in. i'm the last person left in the room.

mad maddie: meet me at back parking lot!

SnowAngel: YEAH!!!

zoegirl: omigosh, maddie. ☹

mad maddie: i know

zoegirl: she's *gone*. she's really gone.

mad maddie: do u have to say it like that?

zoegirl: but it's the truth. as of exactly one hour ago, angela doesn't live here anymore.

mad maddie:	**i don't know how to**
mad maddie:	**i feel so**
zoegirl:	wrong?
mad maddie:	**yeah**
mad maddie:	**w/o her, everything feels wrong**

Sat, Dec 18, 10:21 PM P.S.T.

SnowAngel:	well, here i am in crudballs california. i cldn't txt before now cuz stupid me cldn't find stupid charger and . . . yeah.
SnowAngel:	r u there, zo?
SnowAngel:	ohhhhh. it's, what, after midnight there? so yr probably in bed, while here i am, not even in the same TIME ZONE as u anymore!
SnowAngel:	i hate this so much, zo.
SnowAngel:	and guess what? my bracelet broke. i snagged it on the corner of the ticket counter at the airport, and the leather snapped and the silver part flew off and i couldn't find it anywhere and now it's ruined, just like my whole entire life.
SnowAngel:	so just in case u were wondering, let me enlighten u:
SnowAngel:	i
SnowAngel:	don't
SnowAngel:	b
SnowAngel:	lieve

Sat, Dec 18, 10:33 PM P.S.T.

SnowAngel:	maddie?
SnowAngel:	oh, ma-a-a-a-ddie!
SnowAngel:	great, even UR asleep.
SnowAngel:	i lost my "believe" bracelet. ask zoe, she'll tell u what happened.
SnowAngel:	i want it back, mads.
SnowAngel:	i want my life back.

Sun, Dec 19, 2:11 PM E.S.T.

zoegirl: hey, mads. i talked to angela this morning. she's incredibly sad, big surprise.

mad maddie: fill me in

zoegirl: she hates her apartment, for one thing. and she hates el cerrito.

zoegirl: it's so weird imagining her in a brand-new place. i keep telling myself it's true, but it doesn't *feel* true.

mad maddie: i know what u mean. i drove by her house yesterday, even tho i know i shouldn't have. it looked so . . . empty.

zoegirl: i bet

zoegirl: she told me again how much she loved our moonlight picnic, though. and the photo album. she said looking at it is the only thing keeping her sane.

mad maddie: that was a good time 👍

zoegirl: i don't know if i'd say it was a "good" time, but i know what you mean.

zoegirl: i told you we'd be sobbing, though. even u, miss i'm-so-tough-maddie. sometimes i think you're the biggest softie of us all.

mad maddie: oh please

zoegirl: in a good way!

mad maddie: ok, well, enough of this drama, cuz i'm off to meet chive. wanna come?

zoegirl: no thanks. i guess i feel more like being alone.

mad maddie: u deal with things your way, i'll deal with them mine.

mad maddie: laters!

SnowAngel: maddie maddie maddie! hey, maddie!

mad maddie: a-boogie! wassup?

SnowAngel: FINALLY! omg, i've been trying to reach u forever!

SnowAngel: u haven't been avoiding me, have u?

mad maddie: WHAT?

SnowAngel: u haven't texted me, and u haven't returned my calls. i thought maybe u were sick of me cuz i'm such a downer all the time

mad maddie: don't be crazy—i've just been busy.

mad maddie: so what's new in el cerrito?

SnowAngel: my pillow got lost in the move. isn't that just dandy? the movers arrived this morning, and my pillow wasn't in the truck!

mad maddie: that high-tech squishy pillow from the sleep store?

SnowAngel: it's the only good pillow i've ever had in my life. now i have to use this crap pillow that mom ran out and bought me at some crap store, and it's one more thing in my life that utterly sucks. it's thoroughly and wrongly fluffy, and i'm never gonna be able to sleep again. i just know it. i tried it out on my bed, and i can hear my pulse thru it!

mad maddie: wtf?

SnowAngel: it presses on my neck wrong. it jams up against my carotid artery or whatever the hell it's called, and it makes my pulse ring in my brain. thump! thump! thump! that's all i can hear!

mad maddie: ur losing it, lady

mad maddie: repeat after me, "it is good to have a heartbeat."

SnowAngel: not if u have to HEAR it all the time. i HATE hearing my pulse!

mad maddie: so sleep on your back!

SnowAngel: i can't sleep on my back. i can only sleep on my side.

SnowAngel:	r u purposefully trying to upset me?
mad maddie:	**er, i don't wanna name names, but someone is freaking . . .**
SnowAngel:	*folds arms over chest* zoe would understand.
mad maddie:	**one sec, something just came on tv that i wanna watch**
SnowAngel:	ur watching tv while i pour my heart out? tv's more important than ME?
SnowAngel:	maddie?
SnowAngel:	maddie!!!
mad maddie:	**good god, i just saw THE most horrifying newsclip. u can catch on fire at the gas station if u touch the gas pump with too much static electricity—did u know that? they showed this girl putting the nozzle in her gas tank thingie, and then she got back in her car while it was pumping. she was wearing a sweater, and apparently it rubbed against the seat and got her all staticky. she went back to grab the pump . . . and KAPOW! she burst into flames!**
SnowAngel:	is this supposed to cheer me up? "sorry u lost your pillow, but at least u avoided self-immolation"?
mad maddie:	**sweater girl survived, but the news guy said that other people have actually died.**
mad maddie:	**damn.** 🔥🔥🔥
mad maddie:	**u be careful, u hear?**
SnowAngel:	why do i need to be careful? i don't even have a car. i wanted a car, but instead i got to move to california, remember?
mad maddie:	**well, when and if u DO get a car, don't get back in it while ur in the middle of pumping gas. and touch the side of the car before u grab the gas pump again. that way the static electricity will flow out of u.**

SnowAngel: thanks for the tip *regards friend sourly*

SnowAngel: do u have anything else to say?

**mad maddie: umm . . . don't wear fluffy sweaters when u go to
                the gas station?**

SnowAngel: gbye, maddie!!!

Tues, Dec 21, 10:30 AM E.S.T.

zoegirl: hey, angela. is it too early for me to be texting?
                i can never remember the time difference.

zoegirl: angela?

zoegirl: okay, guess that's a yes. but i just wanted to tell
                u that i mailed you a present today—snail mail!
                old-school!—so you should get it soon, hopefully
                by christmas eve.

zoegirl: i love you, angela! text me!!! 🩶

Wed, Dec 22, 4:43 PM P.S.T.

SnowAngel: hey, zo. sorry i missed u yesterday—i was sleeping in.
                it's like all i do is sleep these days, and i'm STILL tired.

zoegirl: that's okay. i would have called u back last night,
                but i picked up a shift at Kidding Around.

SnowAngel: was doug there?

zoegirl: he was, yeah

SnowAngel: i had a dream about him, isn't that weird? it was
                actually about BOTH of u. u had dyed your hair
                blond to impress him.

SnowAngel: which leads me to ask: u haven't started liking him,
                have u?

zoegirl: *angela*

SnowAngel: i'm sorry, i'm sorry *grimaces*

SnowAngel: why am i so needy? is it just cuz i'm stuck 3,000 miles
                away from u guys, and i feel like everything's being
                torn apart?

zoegirl: you're being silly. nothing's being torn apart.

SnowAngel:	i hope not
SnowAngel:	so have i mentioned that life sucks? i told mom AGAIN that i wanna move back to atlanta and live with my aunt sadie, but she was like, "u haven't given california a chance. ur gonna love it, u'll see."
zoegirl:	maybe you will. i can see you as a california girl, all tan and beautiful. hey—maybe you'll learn to surf!
SnowAngel:	???
SnowAngel:	seriously?
zoegirl:	sorry. just trying to be optimistic.
SnowAngel:	u know what i miss that i didn't even realize i was gonna miss? magnolia trees. i never knew how much i loved them until i moved here.
SnowAngel:	it is a barren wasteland of sadness. that is where i live now. *single tear*
zoegirl:	i love magnolia trees too
SnowAngel:	plus i HATE our apartment. i still have boxes all over my room. isn't that depressing? it's like i can't bear to make myself unpack.
zoegirl:	sorry you hate it, but describe it anyway so i can see you in my mind.
SnowAngel:	it's tiny. it's beige. there's wallpaper in my room with stupid rosebuds on it, and i can hear traffic thru my window. mom says rentals here r super-expensive and we're lucky dad found a three-bedroom place, but i disagree.
zoegirl:	have you met anybody else in the apartment complex?
SnowAngel:	no, and i don't want to. the family below us has a kid, but she's five. she speaks korean.
zoegirl:	she's five years old and she speaks korean? impressive.

SnowAngel:	no, i meant she speaks korean cuz she IS korean.
zoegirl:	oh
zoegirl:	well . . .
SnowAngel:	yes, zoe? if u can put a positive spin on my sucky life, then believe me, i wanna hear it.
zoegirl:	um . . . at least it's almost christmas? 🎄
SnowAngel:	at least it's almost christmas. *sigh*

Thu, Dec 23, 6:02 PM E.S.T.

mad maddie:	dude! chive gave me a nickel bag of pot to celebrate the birth of christ. isn't that righteous?
SnowAngel:	what a guy
SnowAngel:	but don't u think that's sacrilegious?
mad maddie:	i gave him a cool marble pipe i bought at the head store in little five points. oh, and i made him a fantastic playlist that for the record was way more complicated to make than it shld have been. why does iTunes make it so hard to gift playlists instead of individual songs???
mad maddie:	we're gonna make use of it all tomorrow night— if i can escape the fam.
SnowAngel:	maddie, tomorrow's christmas eve. u can't smoke pot on christmas eve!
mad maddie:	why not? the three wise men followed a frickin STAR all the way to Bethlehem. ur telling me they weren't under the influence of a certain illegal substance?
SnowAngel:	tsk, tsk
SnowAngel:	i think u need to start going to church with zoe, young lady!
mad maddie:	yeah, that'll happen
SnowAngel:	does this mean u've learned how to smoke it in a way that doesn't hurt?

mad maddie: i wouldn't say that, exactly. that's why i bought the pipe—it's supposed to make it a smoother ride. but anything'll get better the more u do it, right?

SnowAngel: uh, i guess

mad maddie: it's bound to

mad maddie: btw, chive says u can score some really good pot in california, so keep your eye out for me. 😉 😉

SnowAngel: yeah, that's what i need, to get busted for drugs on top of everything else.

mad maddie: whine, whine, whine. nobody actually gets busted for buying pot. you only get hassled if ur a big-time cocaine dealer or something.

SnowAngel: omg, u haven't tried COCAINE, have u?

mad maddie: angela, chill. pot is my drug of choice, thank u very much.

mad maddie: so check it out: i bought your christmas present, and you are going to LOVE it. wanna know what it is?

SnowAngel: a totally rockin marble pipe?

mad maddie: haha. no, microwavable slippers.

SnowAngel: aw, maddie, thanks! 🙂

SnowAngel: and what, exactly, will i do with these microwavable slippers?

mad maddie: microwave them, of course! the bottoms have these pouches of rice or beans or something in them, and when u microwave them, they get roasty-toasty. they're for cold feet, u goof.

SnowAngel: ooo, they sound wonderful. it gets really chilly here at night, like unbelievably so. and our apartment is always freezing.

mad maddie: i'll put them in the mail tomorrow—that is, unless i don't. but i'll mail them soon, i promise.

SnowAngel: no rush. i haven't even picked out anything for u or zoe.

mad maddie:	**so what's up with zoe these days? i haven't seen her all vacation.**
SnowAngel:	why not?
mad maddie:	**dunno, just haven't. it's not for any BAD reason.**
SnowAngel:	well, she's fine as far as i know. she's working a lot, it sounds like.
SnowAngel:	with doug
mad maddie:	**why do u say it like that, "with doug"?**
SnowAngel:	i dunno. i can't get him out of my mind.
SnowAngel:	u don't think there's anything going on between him and zoe, do u?
mad maddie:	**did zoe say there was?**
SnowAngel:	no, of course not. i'm just being silly.
mad maddie:	**listen, i've g2g. i've gotta stash my pot somewhere so the moms won't find it. i'm thinking the box from the set of "thank u" notes u gave me when we were thirteen. perfect, yeah?**
SnowAngel:	gee, i'm touched
mad maddie:	**why did u give those to me, anyway? i mean, c'mon. thank u notes?**
SnowAngel:	i don't know, cuz they were cute. they were decorated with strawberries.
SnowAngel:	do you have any left?
mad maddie:	**i have every single one of them left, and u know why? cuz they're cute and they're decorated with strawberries, fool.** 😊
mad maddie:	**but the box makes a PERFECT hiding spot for my pot.**
SnowAngel:	cute little strawberries, cute little baggie of pot . . .
mad maddie:	**organic! yeah!**

Fri, Dec 24, 3:33 PM P.S.T.

SnowAngel:	zoe, the pressie u sent me came today! thank u sooooo much!!!

zoegirl:	oh, angela, you are sooooo welcome!
zoegirl:	u like?
SnowAngel:	it's beautiful. SHE'S beautiful, i shld say. i put her on my bedside table so i can see her first thing when i wake up. she's the only decoration in my entire room.
zoegirl:	she's the angel of hope, which you probably already know if you looked at the sticker on the bottom. i know it's dorky, but i thought it could be kind of like your "believe" bracelet, although it's not something to wear.
SnowAngel:	aww, zoe, ur so sweet
zoegirl:	i looked for another "believe" bracelet, by the way. i went to the store where u got it, but i couldn't find anything like it.
SnowAngel:	cuz it was the only 1. ever.
SnowAngel:	but THANK U for my angel. 😇 i love her, love her, love her. *sends big smoochie kisses to dear friend zoe*
zoegirl:	plus, the whole "angel" thing, with you being our SnowAngel and all.
SnowAngel:	she's great, and god knows i need all the angels i can get.
zoegirl:	i almost got one for myself, but then i thought, "no, it should just be something special for angela."
SnowAngel:	we can share her, how bout that?
zoegirl:	yay!
SnowAngel:	so whenever u think of doing something bad, u can remember that she's watching over u from california, and u can change your erring ways? 😇
zoegirl:	haha
zoegirl:	can u believe it's christmas eve?
SnowAngel:	no, i thoroughly cannot. i haven't done ANY shopping, which for my family is just too damn bad. but for u and maddie, i feel terrible.

zoegirl:	please don't, you've got enough to worry about. seriously, we don't care in the slightest.
SnowAngel:	but i do
SnowAngel:	hey, i know! i'll mail ME back to atlanta for your present!
zoegirl:	yeah!!!
SnowAngel:	how much does a plane ticket cost, u think? i've got $250 in savings. is that enough?
zoegirl:	i don't know. i bet it's a little more than that. but maybe?
zoegirl:	are you really thinking about coming?
SnowAngel:	i doubt my parents would let me.
SnowAngel:	but if it's my money, then i can do what i want, right?
zoegirl:	er . . .
SnowAngel:	i'm gonna go check plane fares.
SnowAngel:	don't worry, i'm not REALLY gonna take off w/o my parents' permission, but it would be good info to have in the back of my brain—just in case.
zoegirl:	just in case what?
SnowAngel:	what's that one website called? canoe-something-or-other?
SnowAngel:	i'll figure it out. bye!

Sat, Dec 25, 1:01 PM P.S.T.

SnowAngel:	merry christmas, zoe!!!
zoegirl:	merry christmas! you seem happy. are you happy?
SnowAngel:	i am—or at least this is the happiest i've been since we moved. my mom made cinnamon rolls for breakfast, and our tree looks so beautiful, even tho it's not nearly as big as the one we had last year. and tomorrow we're gonna drive into the city for the after-christmas sales.

zoegirl:	cool
zoegirl:	when you say "the city," do you mean san francisco?
SnowAngel:	yeah, ppl here just call it the city. anyway, we're gonna get a hotel room and stay for a couple of nights, do some of the touristy stuff. so i might be less text-y for a while since my parents hate it when i use my phone when we're supposed to be having QUALITY FAMILY TIME.
zoegirl:	same here, actually. we're going to my grandmom's house tomorrow. we won't be back till wednesday.
SnowAngel:	and maddie's already left for her aunt and uncle's. she was planning on taking her stash with her, did she tell u?
zoegirl:	her "stash"?
zoegirl:	of what?
SnowAngel:	of pot. that's what chive gave her for christmas.
zoegirl:	is she actually gonna *smoke* it?
zoegirl:	oh man, angela. i am not liking this "maddie + pot" combo. i think it's a bad idea. and i think it's a really bad idea that she'd even consider getting high with her family around.
SnowAngel:	she said it's a coping mechanism based on years of family tradition, just that her relatives use alcohol instead of pot. and then she was like, "not that i have anything against alcohol, don't get me wrong . . ."
zoegirl:	you should tell her how dumb she's being
SnowAngel:	what do u mean, *i* should? ur the one who's still in town with her!
zoegirl:	yeah, but *you're* the one she talks to about this stuff. she never brings it up with me.
SnowAngel:	cuz she knows u'd scold her

zoegirl: i bet she's doing it to impress chive, so that when she gets back in town, she can be like, "hey, i smoked the stash u gave me."

SnowAngel: no, here's what she'd say: "duuuuude. good times, buddy. good times."

zoegirl: i don't like it. it worries me.

SnowAngel: it worries me too

SnowAngel: so . . .

zoegirl: so . . . ?

SnowAngel: so we'll tell her, ok?

SnowAngel: for real, w/o holding back

zoegirl: yeah, okay

Thu, Dec 30, 11:33 AM P.S.T.

SnowAngel: madigan, long time no talk! how was your trip?

mad maddie: hey, a. one sec while i finish this email . . .

mad maddie: ok, i'm back. i was responding to a delta airlines customer service dude. alas, still no word on your bracelet.

SnowAngel: u emailed delta about my bracelet? aw, mads!!!!

mad maddie: he checked their claim area, but no "believe" thingie.

SnowAngel: damn

SnowAngel: but that was incredibly sweet of u to try

mad maddie: yeah, i know

SnowAngel: so did u have a good time with your relatives?

mad maddie: the usual. the cousins breathed garlic in my face, the dads got ripped and made fart jokes.

mad maddie: but i wanna hear about U! how was the city?!!

SnowAngel: oh, maddie, it was AWESOME. the only un-awesome thing was that u and zoe weren't there, cuz u guys would have loved it. there's so much going on— omg, it's so different from atlanta. OR el cerrito, which doesn't even compare.

SnowAngel: there was this street musician on the sidewalk who totally made me think of u. he played the guitar, and he had a harmonica on a frame by his mouth, and he had cymbals strapped to his knees. i was like, "maddie would love this guy."

mad maddie: sounds cool. atlanta is pretty boring when it comes to street life.

SnowAngel: san francisco is definitely not boring. there are ppl EVERYWHERE. vendors selling jewelry, hot dog stands, guys with knockoff watches. oh, and we went to chinatown, which was sooooo fun. u go thru this archway thing, and it's like stepping into a different world. everyone was chinese—der—and they had these cute little shops with satin slippers and sparkly barrettes. touristy stuff too, like miniature trolley cars and I 💜 SAN FRANCISCO shirts.

mad maddie: did ya get me 1? did ya, did ya?

SnowAngel: sorry, no tacky souvenir shirt

mad maddie: damn. chive loves that campy stuff.

SnowAngel: i got u something better. i got u lots of stuff, actually—u and zoe both. from chinatown i got u guys candy, like Hello Kitty suckers and gum in weird flavors like cantaloupe and blueberry. and from the ferry building, which is this place down on the waterfront, i got u both boxes of the most awesome chocolates in the world, called Scharffen Berger chocolates. i got u a mix-and-match assortment with infusions of lavender and chile—which sounds gross, but it's not—and i got zoe a box of these super-thin pear slices dipped in dark chocolate. i hope u guys like them.

mad maddie: we will, i'm sure. thanks, a.

SnowAngel: and b-t-dubs, i LOVE my slippers. i've got them on right now.

mad maddie: angela. u do realize that it takes longer to spell out "b-t-dubs" than to just type "by the way," don't you?

SnowAngel: *blinks like a lizard* *like an expressionless lizard*

mad maddie: back to yr slippers. did u microwave them?

SnowAngel: i did. chrissy was like, "ew, what's that smell? it smells like burnt straw!"

mad maddie: hey now—the guy said they were supposed to smell good!

SnowAngel: i like the smell, it's just chrissy who doesn't. anyway it doesn't matter, cuz they feel so lovely and warm. 😍

mad maddie: i'm glad u like them. and i'm glad ur doing better in the land of california.

mad maddie: u are doing better, right?

SnowAngel: i dunno. a LITTLE, i guess.

mad maddie: take it and run with it, girl. u deserve it.

SnowAngel: except school starts on tuesday. that's five days away!

mad maddie: nyah, nyah! u have to start a day earlier than we do!

SnowAngel: i just hope all the girls aren't like glendy. i have to spend tomorrow night with her, cuz mr. boss invited our whole family over for new year's eve, and of course my dad said yes.

SnowAngel: can u imagine a worse way to ring in the new year? i begged my dad to let me stay home, but he refused.

mad maddie: bastard

SnowAngel: what about u? what r u gonna do for new year's?

mad maddie: i'm hanging with my man chive, and probably meade and brannen and whitney. we're going to a concert at the omni. it's a battle of the bands.

SnowAngel: huh. r whitney and chive still an item?

mad maddie: do u know how much he would hate it if he heard u call them that? an "item"?

SnowAngel: so r they?

mad maddie: i guess, altho they can't be THAT serious, cuz sometimes chive and i still fool around. like yesterday we were on a beer run, and at a stoplight he just leaned over and kissed me out of the blue. a LONG kiss.

SnowAngel: and u let him?

mad maddie: what do u mean "let" him?

mad maddie: whitney may be his girlfriend, but that's just cuz . . . i dunno. cuz she's pretty. cuz she does the girl thing and pouts when he doesn't call her. but i'm the one he talks to about music and life and shit. we've got, like, a connection.

SnowAngel: hmmm

SnowAngel: but then—don't be mad—why does he make u hide it?

mad maddie: give me a break. we're not into rules, angela. the world is bigger than that.

SnowAngel: oh

mad maddie: what does that mean?

SnowAngel: nothing!

mad maddie: yes it does. u said it like u don't believe it, i can tell.

SnowAngel: did u smoke the bag of pot he gave u?

mad maddie: as a matter of fact i did. do u have a problem with that too?

mad maddie: it's just POT, angela. nobody's gonna get hurt from a little pot.

SnowAngel: if u say so

SnowAngel: just . . . be careful, all right?

mad maddie: i'm having fun, angela. be happy for me.

SnowAngel: ok, ok

mad maddie: good luck tomorrow night with glendy. call and tell me how it goes!

Fri, Dec 31, 5:30 PM E.S.T.

zoegirl: helloooo! i can't chat for long—i've got to get ready for tonight—but i wanted to talk to u one last time before the new year. is that dorky or what? i'm turning into my grandmom. every year, on the night before my bday, she calls and says, "i just wanted to talk to u one last time while you're __, honey."

SnowAngel: awww

SnowAngel: what r u getting ready for? do u have big new year's eve plans?

zoegirl: oh

zoegirl: um, not really, just a party

SnowAngel: a party? with who?

zoegirl: actually, it's not a party, it's more like people are just going to hang out from work.

zoegirl: it's no big deal

SnowAngel: will doug be there?

zoegirl: huh, i don't know

zoegirl: but i wish i was doing something with *you* instead. you and maddie, that is. like last year when we made chocolate fondue and maddie fondued a tomato. remember?

SnowAngel: u could still do something with her even tho i'm not there.

SnowAngel: why aren't u?

zoegirl: cuz we both have plans already, i guess

SnowAngel: that's lame. have u seen her at all this whole vacation?

zoegirl: well, we've both been out of town

SnowAngel: i talked to her about chive.

zoegirl:	you did? what did she say?
SnowAngel:	she got defensive, and then i felt bad for bringing it up. and then . . . i dunno. i decided to let it go.
zoegirl:	angela!
SnowAngel:	i don't wanna spend my time with her arguing—i get so little time with her as it is.
SnowAngel:	anyway, it's her life. she knows what she's doing.
zoegirl:	does she?
SnowAngel:	as much as any of us, i guess

Sat, Jan 1, 11:34 AM E.S.T.

zoegirl:	mads! happy new year!
mad maddie:	oof, if u say so
mad maddie:	can u txt me later? i'm kinda hurting here.
zoegirl:	hurting how? are you hungover?
mad maddie:	maybe just a tad
zoegirl:	just give me a second. it's important.
mad maddie:	*groans* wassup?
zoegirl:	i have something to tell you, that's all. it's about . . .
mad maddie:	yessss?
zoegirl:	hold on, first let me ask you something. things aren't weird between us, are they?
mad maddie:	huh?
zoegirl:	angela thinks it's strange that we haven't seen each other much over vacation. but that's just because we've been busy, right?
mad maddie:	duh. why else?
zoegirl:	no other reason at all. i just wanted to make sure.
mad maddie:	so what's going on that u need to talk about?
zoegirl:	aaargh. it's about doug. we kind of . . . hung out together last night.
mad maddie:	oh yeah? did u go to a new year's eve party?

zoegirl:	no, it was just the two of us.
mad maddie:	**as in a DATE?**
mad maddie:	**does angela know???**
zoegirl:	er . . . that's part of the problem.
mad maddie:	**yeah, i'll say. angela's gonna think u purposely waited till she was gone, and then BAM! u stole her man.**
zoegirl:	he's not "her man." sheesh!
mad maddie:	**well, is he YOUR man?**
zoegirl:	that's the other part of the problem. because i don't know, maddie. i just don't know!
mad maddie:	**explain**
zoegirl:	we went to dinner at La Fonda, and that was great. i love their guacamole. and then neither of us wanted to go home, so we went and hung out in the basement of trinity church. doug's an acolyte, so he's got the key to the youth group lounge.
mad maddie:	**oh god, zoe. again?**
zoegirl:	what do u mean, again?
mad maddie:	**this doesn't ring any bells for u? any CHURCH bells, per chance?**
zoegirl:	what are you talking about?
mad maddie:	**oh, nothing. definitely not a certain holy-roller teacher of yore . . .**
zoegirl:	do u wanna hear my story or not?
mad maddie:	**by all means, pray continue**
zoegirl:	we were sitting there talking, and it was chilly, so doug told me to come sit on the couch with him because it would be warmer. so i did, and . . . we kissed.
mad maddie:	**holy cow**
zoegirl:	that's not all. we *kept* kissing . . . and kissing and kissing and kissing. and it's not like i was swept away or anything, but at the same time i

	didn't stop him, you know? i didn't want to hurt his feelings.
mad maddie:	**u didn't wanna hurt his feelings? u did NOT just say that, zoe.**
zoegirl:	anyway, we somehow ended up with both our shirts practically off, but not completely. they were just pushed up really high.
zoegirl:	actually, i was wearing a sweatshirt—and i wasn't wearing a bra underneath. it was thick enough that i didn't need to! i didn't *expect* anyone to find out!
mad maddie:	**whoa, zoe! u hussy!**
zoegirl:	i know! i'm sure he was pretty startled. but i didn't *plan* it that way—it just happened!
mad maddie:	**and in the church basement, no less. what is it with u and jesus? does he, like, turn u on?**
zoegirl:	can we let go of that, please? i knew you would have to say that, and now you have, so that's over.
mad maddie:	**first mr. h, now doug . . . u give religion a whole new meaning. "hussies for christ"!**
zoegirl:	what if doug *does* think i'm a hussy? what if he woke up this morning and was like, "there's something wrong with her"?
zoegirl:	we did more last night than i've ever done with *anyone*. what if he looks down on me now?
mad maddie:	**zoe, u r so insane i can hardly stand it. i'm sure he went home with a stiffie, while visions of zoe danced in his head.**
zoegirl:	i just wish i didn't feel guilty. why do i feel guilty?!
mad maddie:	**i have nooooo idea. all u did is fool around.**
mad maddie:	**ooo, do u think u made his scrotum tighten?**
zoegirl:	*what*?
mad maddie:	**chive's been reading james joyce, and apparently**

	there's something in one of the books about some guy's scrotum tightening. it cracked me up.
zoegirl:	okay, please do not talk about that particular part of the body in reference to doug ever again, all right?
mad maddie:	doug has a scrotum, doug has a scrotum!
zoegirl:	i mean it, maddie
mad maddie:	cuz u think it's DIRTY? cuz u think it's NASTY?
mad maddie:	zoe, u need to learn how to relax if ur gonna have a boyfriend.
zoegirl:	i don't think any of those things. i just think that not everything is a joke, and that fooling around should count for something. it shouldn't be a free-for-all.
zoegirl:	maybe that's something *you* need to learn if *you're* ever going to have a boyfriend.
zoegirl:	maddie? you still there?
mad maddie:	nothing like a cold dose of reality from one of your best friends, eh, zo?
zoegirl:	maddie . . .
mad maddie:	no need to hold back, u know. just tell me how u really feel.
zoegirl:	look, u started it.
zoegirl:	but i didn't tell u about doug so that you and i could get into a fight. i told you because of *angela*. what am i supposed to do about angela?
mad maddie:	two words, zoe, and i've said 'em before: TELL HER, U IDIOT.
zoegirl:	that's four words
mad maddie:	i'm giving u the bird, just so u know
zoegirl:	ack—she's calling me right now!! i'm not ready to talk to her, so i'm going to turn my phone off and hide it. bye!

SnowAngel: hola, maddie. happy new year!

mad maddie: same to u, a-boogie

SnowAngel: do u know where zo is, by any chance? just called her but went to voicemail.

mad maddie: huh, fancy that

SnowAngel: oh well. i'll try her again later.

SnowAngel: how was your new year's eve??? any smoochy-smoochy action with chive???

mad maddie: ixnay on the oochie-smoochy-say . . . at least b/w me and chive. altho SOMEONE was smoochy-smoochy-ing last night, i can tell u that.

SnowAngel: oh yeah? who?

mad maddie: er . . . no one in particular. i just mean that surely someone was getting it on, cuz after all it was new year's eve, right?

SnowAngel: r u just being random? cuz sometimes i don't know what ur talking about.

mad maddie: forget it. yeah, i was being random.

SnowAngel: so how was the concert?

mad maddie: the bands sucked, but we had a blast. this one band played a cover of "stairway to heaven" and we turned on the flashlights on our phones and waved them over our heads like lighters.

SnowAngel: aw, fun

mad maddie: by the end of the song u could see glowing lights from one end of the amphitheater to the other. it was pretty cool.

mad maddie: also, chive bought us all beers with his fake, so we were verrrrry happy. at least until chive spilled his on the guy in front of us, who happened to be bald. the guy whipped around all mad and fuming, and i was like, "oh shit! sorry, man!"

SnowAngel: what did chive do?

mad maddie: he just sat there cracking up. i was elbowing him and going, "dude, U spilled it!" but he fully let me take the blame. it was hilarious.

SnowAngel: oh yeah. it sounds hilarious. *deadpans to show hilarity*

mad maddie: but i'm hurting today, i'll tell u.

SnowAngel: well, that's too bad

SnowAngel: but i don't feel sorry for u, wanna know why? cuz while u were out whupping it up with chive, i was trapped in glendy's room watching "The Sisterhood of the Traveling Pants" on netflix.

mad maddie: wowzers. dipping into the oldies, huh?

mad maddie: but i thought u liked that movie

SnowAngel: i do!

SnowAngel: but only with u and zoe. i mean, c'mon. four girls, friends forever? that's US, except with three instead of four.

mad maddie: and we're cooler. and we say words like "fuck."

SnowAngel: u, maybe. zoe and i r more refined. *adopts snooty expression and sips from teacup*

mad maddie: fuck, fuck, fuck

SnowAngel: but it wasn't just the choice of movie, altho that WAS the most horrible awful irony imaginable. it was the fact that glendy was such a baby the whole night. they didn't have any popcorn, so she asked her mom if she'd go to the store and buy some. her mom said no, so she worked up these fake tears and tried again with her dad. she was all, "oh, daddy, please? i REALLY need popcorn when i watch a movie. and my friend's here, and she needs popcorn too. please, daddy, please?"

mad maddie: and her dad gave in? bad move, buster.

SnowAngel: i know. she is such an only child.

mad maddie: ha. like zoe?

SnowAngel:	no, cuz zoe's parents r strict.
SnowAngel:	i guess it's possible that glendy's mom is too, but it makes no difference since mr. boss gives in whenever she pretends to cry.
mad maddie:	**and yr sure she's 16 and not 6?**
SnowAngel:	omg, exactly!
SnowAngel:	she kept talking through the whole movie—of course she's a movie-talker—and she was like, "i'm lena, the beautiful one. she's so me."
SnowAngel:	and i was like, "uh, no, ur bailey, the annoying kid who leeched onto tibby. only bailey turned out to be cool, and u r the epitome of uncool."
mad maddie:	**maybe glendy'll get a terminal disease like bailey did**
SnowAngel:	maddie!
mad maddie:	**those sisterhood chicks wouldn't say that either, i know. but it made u laugh, didn't it?**
SnowAngel:	anyway, i couldn't get away from glendy fast enough. and yet, this is who i get to go to school with on tuesday, cuz maddie, we're CARPOOLING!!! mr. boss is gonna drop us off each morning so my mom can drive chrissy to junior high.
mad maddie:	**yuck**
mad maddie:	**u better just move back here. hop on that plane like u said.**
SnowAngel:	plane fares cost more than i thought. 😠 the cheapest was $454, which is $200 too much. *grrr*
mad maddie:	**that sucks**
SnowAngel:	maybe i should ask glendy for a loan, or rather, get her to ask her daddy for 1. what do u think?
mad maddie:	**i think u need to give the glendinizer the boot. just quit talking to her. she'll get the message.**
SnowAngel:	like i can do that when we're squished together in the same car every freakin morning.

mad maddie: oh—i have to tell u one more funny thing that happened at the concert. whitney and i had to pee, but the line in the ladies' room was ridiculously long as usual. so whitney starts whining about how she REALLY has to go, and i'm like, "what do u want me to do about it?" she goes, "i dunno. something!" so i clapped my hands super loud and said, "listen up, ladies. ten seconds apiece! that's your limit!"

SnowAngel: oh god

SnowAngel: and how did u enforce this limit?

mad maddie: i started counting down from 10 to 1 each time someone stepped into a stall. at first ppl just stared at me, but then this big ol' trucker gal with a beer belly started chanting with me, and then other ppl in the line joined in too.

SnowAngel: did it work?

mad maddie: that was the best part! girls started charging out of the stalls with their pants unzipped, trying to beat the clock. one woman yelled, "i need 20! i had dinner at Max's Burritos!"

SnowAngel: good lord

mad maddie: heh heh heh

SnowAngel: i hope whitney appreciated your gesture of goodwill.

mad maddie: r u kidding? she was mortified. AND she took longer than her allotted 10 seconds. she got booed by trucker gal.

SnowAngel: ha!

SnowAngel: i can so see that whole scene. it makes me miss u, mads.

mad maddie: i miss u 2, a

SnowAngel: it's not fair that i have to spend new year's day alone

mad maddie:	**well, do something nice for yourself.**
SnowAngel:	like what?
mad maddie:	**i dunno, whatever u feel like doing. and now i've g2g, cuz it's time for a little nappie. byeas!**

Sat, Jan 1, 4:42 PM P.S.T.

SnowAngel:	zoe, where r u? and why is yr phone turned off??? i can't get hold of u no matter how hard i try!
SnowAngel:	it's the beginning of a new year, and i want to TALK to u.
SnowAngel:	*pouts*
SnowAngel:	fine. i am gonna take maddie's advice and do something fun for a change. i've snagged a bottle of the champagne mom and dad bought for last night—don't worry, it's mini-size, just right for me!—and i'm going to hide out in my room and watch "pitch perfect" and laugh and cry.
SnowAngel:	i just wish u and mads were here to watch it with me!

Sat, Jan 1, 6:01 PM P.S.T.

SnowAngel:	zooo-eeee! oh, zoooo-eeee! where r u, girl?
SnowAngel:	seriously? yr seriously still gon?
SnowAngel:	*gone, sorry. new thumbs, tee hee. i think i'm a little tipsy.
SnowAngel:	AND ALSO I NEED SOMEONE TO KISS!!! BECAUSE THE KISS AT THE END OF PITCH PERFECT IS SO PERFECT!
SnowAngel:	wait! so *pitch* perfect, hahahaha!
SnowAngel:	so, hypothetically, do u think doug would kiss me, if he were here? i think he would. i even thought about kissing him before i left. did u know that?
SnowAngel:	hmm, i think i'll give him a ring-a-ling. *wink, wink*

zoegirl: oh crap. oh crap crap crap!

zoegirl: have you talked to angela today?

mad maddie: **yesterday, but not today. why?**

zoegirl: did you tell her about me and doug? and don't lie!

mad maddie: **chill! i didn't tell her, i swear.**

zoegirl: then how did she know? why did she pick last night, of all the nights in the world, to suddenly ring doug up and offer herself to him? huh???

mad maddie: **what r u talking about?**

zoegirl: she drank some champagne and got all sappy watching "Pitch Perfect," from what i can tell. and then she called up doug, out of the blue, and said things like, "hey, doug. do you miss me? because i miss you!" and "if you were here, i would kiss you. i should have a long time ago!"

mad maddie: **how do u know all this?**

mad maddie: **oh. cuz doug told u.**

mad maddie: **this is NOT good**

zoegirl: you think?

zoegirl: and now doug's all weirded out because it was obvious to him that angela didn't know about us, because if she did then why would she be hitting on him, and he doesn't understand why i haven't told her.

zoegirl: and angela . . . well, who knows how she's doing.

zoegirl: crap, crap, crap!

mad maddie: **i warned u that this was gonna happen. u know i did.**

zoegirl: could u possibly say something the least bit supportive? i didn't plan this. it just happened!

mad maddie: **sure, that's what U say, cuz ur the one who screwed up. can i just tell u how happy i am that it's u for once and not me?**

zoegirl:	you know what? you're not helping. it's like . . . it's like you're *enjoying* this!
mad maddie:	**i'm not "enjoying" it, zoe. get real.**
zoegirl:	i've got to go. this is so messed up.
mad maddie:	**wait! what did doug say to angela after she threw herself at him? u never told me!**
zoegirl:	and i'm not going to. you'd just find some way to make fun of me.
mad maddie:	**zoe!!!!!!**

zoegirl:	hi, angela. it's me, your friend, who is so so sorry about . . . u know.
zoegirl:	i saw your tweet about how california sucks, but at least it isn't full of big fat liars. i assume i'm the big fat liar you're talking about?
zoegirl:	but angela . . .
zoegirl:	aaargh
zoegirl:	i should have told you about me and doug. i know that. but i just . . . i don't know.
zoegirl:	anyway, nothing *had* happened between doug and me when you and i talked about it, so i wasn't actually lying. and the only reason i didn't mention it later is because i didn't wanna hurt you.
zoegirl:	and come on, if you hadn't been so jealous in the first place . . .
zoegirl:	never mind
zoegirl:	i'm sorry, angela. i really am.

SnowAngel:	i just got the lamest series of texts from zoe, which of course i didn't bother to reply to. did she tell u what happened? with doug?

mad maddie: yes, she told me that u've been a very naughty girl. did u drink and dial, young lady????

SnowAngel: WHAT?

SnowAngel: this is NOT about me. it's about ZOE! i'm never gonna forgive her as long as i live.

mad maddie: well, we both know that's not true. but we can pretend if you like.

SnowAngel: i'm serious, maddie. she's all, "i didn't wanna hurt u, blah, blah, blah," but come on. am i so needy and pathetic that i can't even handle the truth?

mad maddie: hmm. do u really want me to answer that?

SnowAngel: she even had the nerve to blame it on me! cuz i was "jealous," and that's why she didn't tell me about her and doug. is that not the most ridiculous thing u've ever heard?

mad maddie: yes, it's the most ridiculous thing i've ever heard, and yes, she should have told u. i told her that a thousand times. and now she's completely freaked that ur mad, but i told her, "sorry, zo, u brought it on yourself."

SnowAngel: thank u. i needed to hear that. i mean, it would have been different if

SnowAngel: wait a minute—U knew too?

mad maddie: about zoe and doug? uh . . .

SnowAngel: u knew they were a couple and u didn't tell me?!!!!

SnowAngel: omg, how long has this been going on???

mad maddie: now listen. IT WASN'T MY PLACE TO TELL. i told zoe she was screwing up, but that was her decision. i'm not her mommy, angela. i'm not either of your mommies.

SnowAngel: nice, maddie. try and shift the responsibility. do u not have any conscience at all?

SnowAngel: obviously not, or u wld have told your best friend that yr other best friend was dating a certain person who someone else still happened to like!

mad maddie: **that's crap, angela. u didn't like doug. u just liked him liking u.**

SnowAngel: that's so not true! why is everybody ganging up on me?

SnowAngel: i told zoe i was glad i moved to california, and guess what? i thoroughly and completely mean it!

Sun, Jan 2, 11:45 AM E.S.T.

mad maddie: **well, i talked to angela.**

zoegirl: and?!!

mad maddie: **she's mad as hell. ur at the top of her shit list, my friend.**

zoegirl: ah, crap.

zoegirl: i'm so stupid! stupid, stupid, stupid!

mad maddie: **no comment**

mad maddie: **r u ever gonna tell me what doug said to her, after she said all that about kissing him?**

zoegirl: he got really nervous, that's all. he blurted out something like, "angela, i'm dating zoe. didn't she tell u?"

mad maddie: **he said that out loud? that u 2 r dating?**

zoegirl: well, yeah. and that part was totally sweet. but i doubt it made angela feel any better, since even he assumed i'd told her.

mad maddie: **u r so screwed**

zoegirl: i know

mad maddie: **well, nothing i can do about it. i'm off to meet chive. laters!**

Mon, Jan 3, 3:30 PM E.S.T.

zoegirl: angela, are you ready to talk to me yet?

zoegirl: angela, come on. i know you're there. and don't

you remember when maddie stonewalled us like this last year, after everything fell apart with jana? i can't believe you're doing the same thing.

zoegirl: *please* don't be this way.

zoegirl: call me!!!

Mon, Jan 3, 6:01 PM P.S.T.

SnowAngel: hi, mads. i am SO not psyched to be me right now.

mad maddie: why? cuz yr still feuding with zoe?

SnowAngel: god, who even cares

SnowAngel: but yeah, i guess so, if by that u mean am i still mad at her. altho what makes me even madder is that i don't WANT to be mad at her. how pathetic is that?

mad maddie: why don't u wanna be mad anymore?

SnowAngel: cuz even tho i hate her right now, i miss her too. *scowls and kicks over trash can*

mad maddie: so get over yourself, freak. u BOTH need to get over yourselves.

SnowAngel: whatever

SnowAngel: anyway, tomorrow's my 1st day at El Cerrito High. i'm nervous.

mad maddie: don't be. u'll be fine.

SnowAngel: what if no one likes me? what if no one talks to me?

mad maddie: well, there's always glendy. maybe u'll have adjoining lockers.

SnowAngel: oh thx

SnowAngel: it's so unfair that i have to be starting over in my junior year.

mad maddie: i agree. u belong back here with us.

SnowAngel: IS there still an "us"?

mad maddie: wtf?

SnowAngel: u and me and zoe. are we still an "us"?

SnowAngel: nvm

SnowAngel:	so what shld i wear tomorrow??? shld i be cool and casual or sleek and sophisticated?
mad maddie:	**christ, angela, i don't know. wear whatever u want.**
SnowAngel:	when we were in the city, my mom bought me this off-the-shoulder sweater that i wear with a tank top underneath. i call it my slutwear, cuz it's pretty tight. and cuz of the shoulder thing. do u think i have good shoulders?
mad maddie:	**uh . . .**
SnowAngel:	she also bought me this fuzzy white sweater with three-quarter-length sleeves. i call that one my kate upton sweater cuz it makes my boobs look ginormous. (well, ginormous for a 34B)
mad maddie:	**good god**
SnowAngel:	so which should i wear??? cuz even tho my life sucks, i do wanna make a good impression.
mad maddie:	**a slutty impression?**
SnowAngel:	NO. *narrows eyes* hot, but classy. not like a woman of the night.
mad maddie:	**zoe's worried that doug thinks she's a woman of the night. isn't that hysterical? apparently the two of them got down and dirty in doug's church's basement, and things went further than zoe intended.**
SnowAngel:	maddie!
SnowAngel:	stop and think for one single second. do u really think i wanna hear this?
mad maddie:	**ur telling me u don't?**
SnowAngel:	just how down and dirty did they get? and why were they in the church basement?
mad maddie:	**i thought u didn't wanna hear!**
SnowAngel:	i don't. *puts hands over ears*
SnowAngel:	it's just, why is he getting down and dirty with zoe instead of me?

mad maddie: why do u think? cuz u never acted the slightest bit interested in him until after zoe got interested. that's why this whole fight is so ridiculous.

SnowAngel: okay. awesome. thx for nothing!!!

Mon, Jan 3, 9:55 PM E.S.T.

mad maddie: ok, angela, here's something to cheer u up. it's Professor Poopypants' Name Change-O-Chart 2000. u type in your name and it spits back your new "silly" name. wanna hear yours?

SnowAngel: is this your peace offering?

mad maddie: your silly name is "stinky pizzabuns," and i'm "pinky pottybutt." i love it.

SnowAngel: not that i care . . . but what's zoe's?

mad maddie: she's got the best of all. "zsa zsa toiletsniffer."

SnowAngel: hmmph

SnowAngel: should i introduce myself tomorrow as "stinky pizzabuns," do u think?

mad maddie: angela, that would be so awesome. u should, u totally should!

SnowAngel: uh . . . no

mad maddie: why not? it's a chance to be a whole new u!

SnowAngel: i don't wanna be a whole new me! i just wanna be the normal old me, but how can i do that if no one even knows who i am?!!

Mon, Jan 3, 10:00 PM E.S.T.

mad maddie: zsa zsa, hey. i just talked to angela, and she is seriously un-stoked about her new school.

zoegirl: maddie! i'm so glad u texted. i've been feeling lonely. but why did u call me zsa zsa?

mad maddie: no reason. so when r u guys gonna get over this stupid fight?

zoegirl: *i'm* not fighting. *she* is. and you're right, it's stupid. i left her a message on her voicemail earlier today, and i was like, "angela, come on. in the grand scheme of things, this is not that big a deal."

mad maddie: **i bet that made her feel validated**

zoegirl: i just meant that our friendship is stronger than this. and i've sent her tons of emails, since she won't respond to my texts or my calls.

mad maddie: **she's weakening. i can tell.**

zoegirl: i dunno, but i hope so. guess i'll try her again tomorrow.

Tues, Jan 4, 4:37 PM P.S.T.

SnowAngel: I HATE EL CERRITO HIGH SO MUCH!!!

mad maddie: **ah, shit. what happened, a?**

SnowAngel: they have METAL DETECTORS, maddie. everyone has to line up and walk thru this security gate, with an armed guard standing right there. it is so so so different from atlanta. it's terrible. 😔

mad maddie: **ick, that would freak me out.**

SnowAngel: and they've got all these stupid rules, like "4 Bs and a U"

mad maddie: **wtf?**

SnowAngel: it's their dress code. no breasts, bellies, backs, or butts, and no underwear. meaning, u can't have any of those things exposed. this guy in my homeroom goes, "it's like we're under control of Al-Qaeda, man." and my homeroom teacher, whom i hate, goes, "yes, only we won't skin u alive. the word for that is 'flay,' by the way."

SnowAngel: what a wanker

mad maddie: **what about the kids? u meet anyone cool?**

SnowAngel: no. not a single person talked to me except glendy

(who was wearing high-rise jeans, fyi) (ALSO, fyi,
while I know that some ppl claim that high-rise
is back in . . . NO. not on glendy.) she glommed
onto me like we were best buds, and i could see
everyone looking at me and going, "L-O-S-E-R."
puts L on forehead

mad maddie: **u've gotta ditch the glendinizer, angela**

SnowAngel: yeah, but how???

SnowAngel: she gave me a little plastic Care Bear to clip
onto my backpack! i tried to stuff it in the bottom
compartment, and she pulled it right back out
again and clipped it onto the zipper!

mad maddie: **egad**

mad maddie: **which care bear is it?**

SnowAngel: Friend Bear!

SnowAngel: SHE IS NOT MY FRIEND!!!

mad maddie: **lose the glendinizer, that's all i can say**

SnowAngel: gee, thanks, ur a big help

mad maddie: **chin up, angela. this was only your first day—**
things'll get better.

SnowAngel: if they don't, i don't know what i'll do

mad maddie: **well, were there any cute guys?**

SnowAngel: no

mad maddie: **any fun teachers?**

SnowAngel: no

mad maddie: **any good snack machines, for god's sake?**

SnowAngel: they sell apples and raisins and granola bars,
maddie. *bares teeth in horrid semblance of a
smile*

mad maddie: **no licorice whips? no devilishly good ding dongs?**

SnowAngel: it's meant to stimulate better brain growth. freakin
california!

mad maddie: **ok, now ur depressing ME**

SnowAngel: as if my life wasn't bad enough, i have to read three chapters of biology and write a response to the first 20 pages of "The Heart of Darkness." *glowers* I'LL show 'em a heart of darkness.

mad maddie: the horror! the horror!

Wed, Jan 5, 7:45 PM E.S.T.

zoegirl: hi, angela. everyone missed you at school today, just so you know. especially me.

Wed, Jan 5, 4:45 PM P.S.T.

SnowAngel: ok, i've decided to talk to u. but i'm still extremely mad.

zoegirl: angela!

zoegirl: hurray, hurray, hurray!

SnowAngel: i TOLD u, i'm still mad at u.

zoegirl: i know, and i totally deserve it. and if it makes you feel any better, doug was mad at me too. we, like, had our first fight.

SnowAngel: how tragic—by which i mean "yay."

SnowAngel: u fought over me?

zoegirl: well, we didn't exactly fight, and it wasn't exactly over you. i mean, not in *that* way. but he thought i'd put you in a really bad position by not telling you about the two of us, and that by doing that, i put him in a really bad position.

zoegirl: neither of us meant to hurt your feelings, angela

SnowAngel: *glares silently*

zoegirl: please don't be mad anymore. i just got caught in my own stupidness, that's all. i really did think you didn't like him, because that's what you've always said.

zoegirl: do you forgive me?

SnowAngel: no

SnowAngel:	but one day if u text me again, maybe i'll text back. and if u call my cell, i MIGHT pick up.
zoegirl:	well . . . that's a start, i guess
SnowAngel:	only i've had enough for right now, cuz u shouldn't get off scot-free after being such a jerk. so, good-bye.
zoegirl:	angela . . .
zoegirl:	are you serious?
zoegirl:	ok, fine. but come back soon!!!

Thu, Jan 6, 6:04 PM P.S.T.

SnowAngel:	hi, zoe
zoegirl:	angela, hi! you DID text me back, you did! what's up?
SnowAngel:	nothing, except i guess i wanna say that i forgive u for real.
zoegirl:	you do? thank god!
SnowAngel:	my mom says it was a coping strategy to be so angry at u, that it gave me something to focus all my anger at. i can't control being stuck in california, but i CLD control being mad at u.
zoegirl:	huh
zoegirl:	i did kind of wonder if u were taking things out on me . . . but i also know that i really did screw up.
SnowAngel:	u got that right
zoegirl:	and like i said, i'm sorry
SnowAngel:	*deep, cleansing breath* and i forgive u
SnowAngel:	so now u have to tell me about him, since u didn't for all this time.
zoegirl:	who, doug?
SnowAngel:	no, benedict cumberbatch. of course doug!!!
zoegirl:	well . . . he's wonderful. he's funny and he's sweet and he's got a poster of kermit the frog in his room.
zoegirl:	are you sure u want to hear this?

SnowAngel:	no, turns out i don't
SnowAngel:	just tell me 1 thing. do u honestly like him? like, a lot?
zoegirl:	yeah . . . i do.
SnowAngel:	why? i'm not being a brat, i really wanna know.
zoegirl:	oh, angela
zoegirl:	i like him because when we talk, it feels real. like, last night we sat on the floor of the den and watched this candle burn down, and we talked about all kinds of things—our families, what we want to do when we're older, what we believe in terms of God.
zoegirl:	it's just so rare to find someone—a guy!—who gets me, you know? who doesn't make me feel fake when i say what i'm honestly thinking.
SnowAngel:	yeah, i can see that
zoegirl:	although then it was weird when we finally stopped talking and it was time for him to go. he kept jingling his keys, but he wouldn't get up from the sofa and walk out the door. because i guess he was . . . thinking we should fool around.
SnowAngel:	what???
zoegirl:	never mind, that just slipped out. i didn't mean to bring up a touchy subject.
SnowAngel:	too late now. tell me!
zoegirl:	you sure?
SnowAngel:	if u don't, it will just make things worse.
zoegirl:	well, on our 1st date we fooled around kind of more than we should have, maybe. only why do i feel like that? like we *shouldn't* have? tons of people fool around. maddie fools around all the time. so if doug and i want to fool around, we should, right?
SnowAngel:	is this my little zoe, all grown up? should i be putting on my mom's "Fiddler on the Roof" cd? *strikes

	melancholy pose* "Is this the little girl I carried? Is this the little boy at play? I don't remember growing older. When did they?"
zoegirl:	are you making fun of me?
SnowAngel:	"Sunrise, sunset. Sunrise, sunset. Swiftly flow the days!"
zoegirl:	stop singing!!!!!!!
SnowAngel:	ok, let's recap. u got down and dirty on your first date, and last night doug wanted an instant replay. did u give him one or not?
zoegirl:	*not*
zoegirl:	we kissed, but i didn't let it go further than that. finally i said, "doug, we have to get some sleep. you have to go." he didn't take the hint, so i pulled him up and propelled him to the door and very unsubtly pushed him toward his car.
zoegirl:	now i'm worried he thought i was being a jerk.
SnowAngel:	yeah, he probably did
SnowAngel:	jk
zoegirl:	i didn't know it would be this complicated. the physical stuff, i mean.
SnowAngel:	just remember that as much as it pains me to say this, it really is ok to fool around or kiss or whatever. as long as you like each other, then that's a GOOD thing.
zoegirl:	i know
SnowAngel:	and there's a difference b/w fooling around and hooking up.
SnowAngel:	ur not maddie, zoe. don't worry.
zoegirl:	ouch
zoegirl:	but thanks. i know this can't be the easiest thing for you to talk about.
SnowAngel:	get real. what kind of twisted friend would freak out over a guy she'd never even gone out with???

SnowAngel:	anyway, that's what i'm here for, even if i AM 3,000 miles away.
zoegirl:	wait! we forgot to talk about YOU! do you want to tell me about your new school?
SnowAngel:	nah, i'm pretty wiped. i'm just glad things r good b/w us.
zoegirl:	me too. night!

Fri, Jan 7, 6:50 PM E.S.T.

mad maddie:	u know what i hate? ppl who hate everyone. ppl who walk around so wrapped up in their own bullshit that they can't possibly imagine that everyone else might NOT be as fake as they wanna think they r.
SnowAngel:	and hello to u 2. what r u going on about?
mad maddie:	just cuz i don't wear all black, that makes me a sellout? that automatically implies that i worship taylor swift?
SnowAngel:	i like taylor swift. she's amazing.
mad maddie:	don't tell katie thompson and her minions that. they were trolling the halls today in their black eyeliner and their "wacky" clothes, and all i cld think was, "god, i'm sick of school already, and i've only been back three days." the katies think they're so DIFFERENT, but they can only be different in a group. have u noticed?
SnowAngel:	i did back in the good old days, yes. but in case u've forgotten, katie and i no longer live in the same state.
mad maddie:	i know that. DER.
mad maddie:	i just mean that if ur gonna be different, u should be different for real, not cuz of some bullshit desire to be different. like—well, hold on, chive says it better than me. here, this is from his deadjournal:

Chet Baker is the man. Never learned to read music, because he heard the music in his soul. Lived hard and fast, because that's what living is for. He lost his teeth in a street fight, but still he was the best jazz trumpet player this world has ever seen. The prince of cool.

Check it out, from "Chet Baker's Unsung Swan Song" by David Wilcox:

My old addiction
Makes me crave only what is best
Like these just this morning song birds
Craving upward from the nest.

mad maddie: **doesn't that say it all?**

SnowAngel: i don't get it. who's chet baker?

mad maddie: **just the best trumpet player ever. it says it right there.**

SnowAngel: what's the bit about the birds craving upward from the nest? is it poetry?

mad maddie: **it's a SONG by david wilcox. don't u know who david wilcox is?**

SnowAngel: no

SnowAngel: did U, pre-chive?

mad maddie: **it's about how chet b. died by falling out of a hotel window. he was wasted, apparently. hence, like a bird leaning out of its nest.**

SnowAngel: a bird that was wasted?

mad maddie: **the point is that chet baker lived his life on his own terms, unlike katie thompson. he took risks. he was unpredictable.**

SnowAngel: u don't have to be wasted to be unpredictable. i'm not goth or emo or anything, and I'M unpredictable.

mad maddie:	**U? hahahahahaha**
mad maddie:	**i love u, angela, but ur as predictable as they come. type in "16-year-old girl" and out pops "angela silver."**
SnowAngel:	excuse me? name ONE thing about me that's predictable!
mad maddie:	**uh, let's c. your ryan gosling obsession? your need to shop? and let's not forget the fight ur having with zoe, which is over the most predictable thing in the world—a guy.**
SnowAngel:	what fight? we worked things out.
mad maddie:	**come again?**
SnowAngel:	i still think she handled everything completely wrong . . . but MAYBE i shouldn't have made such a case out of her hanging out with doug. maybe i sorta knew that she liked him all along.
mad maddie:	**oh**
mad maddie:	**that doesn't make it ok, tho. she LIED to u.**
SnowAngel:	i know she did
mad maddie:	**more than once, i might add.**
SnowAngel:	what's your point? do u not want me to forgive her?
mad maddie:	**no, i do. of course i do.**
SnowAngel:	good, cuz i did
SnowAngel:	and u wanna know what's weird? it was a total power trip to let her off the hook. i didn't know it was gonna be, but it was. it was such a role reversal— the great zoe messing up!
SnowAngel:	does that make any sense?
mad maddie:	**you got to be the magnanimous one. you got to choose whether to let her live or die.**
SnowAngel:	yeah. i'm not saying i'm glad it happened . . . but part of me liked having her grovel.
mad maddie:	**i can totally understand**
SnowAngel:	plus, what else was i supposed to do?

SnowAngel:	she's my zoe, just like ur my maddie. i can't live w/o either of u.
mad maddie:	**lucky for u, u don't have to.**
SnowAngel:	which is good, cuz now i won't have to get wasted and fall out a hotel window.
mad maddie:	**haha, very funny!**

Sat, Jan 8, 11:45 AM E.S.T.

zoegirl:	wake up, angela! wake up, wake up!
SnowAngel:	*rubs sleep from eyes* it's not noon here, zoe. we're three hours earlier, remember?
zoegirl:	oh yeah, i forgot
zoegirl:	so that makes it . . . 8:45? wow, ur up early.
SnowAngel:	*smiles wanly*
zoegirl:	so what's going on? you have any big plans for tonight?
SnowAngel:	no, cuz i have no friends, cuz apparently i suck.
zoegirl:	what about glendy?
SnowAngel:	haha. glendy is WORSE than no friends.
SnowAngel:	yesterday she cornered me at lunch and made me go to the bathroom with her. she needed me to run the water in the sink while she . . . did her business. what a baby!
zoegirl:	why run water?
zoegirl:	ohhhhh. to cover the sounds?
SnowAngel:	she doesn't want anyone to hear her peeing. isn't that something ur supposed to be over by the time ur 16? i was like, "we ALL do it, glendy. every single 1 of us pees, even mother teresa."
zoegirl:	i have a hard time peeing around other people too, though. in my head i'm like, "just pee, just pee!" but sometimes my body refuses to cooperate.
zoegirl:	oh gosh. does that mean i'm repressed?
SnowAngel:	huh?

zoegirl:	maddie thinks i am. she says i'm a prude.
SnowAngel:	no offense, but compared to maddie, anyone would be a prude
SnowAngel:	oops *claps hand over mouth*
zoegirl:	sometimes i worry she's right, though. like with doug, i still get nervous about all the body stuff. i can never just let go and enjoy it, not all the way.
zoegirl:	am i allowed to talk to you about this? i don't wanna make you feel bad.
SnowAngel:	the only time u make me feel bad is when u say things like "i don't wanna make u feel bad."
SnowAngel:	so when u say u can't just let go and enjoy it . . . does that mean things have been progressing?
zoegirl:	well, doug wants them to. i keep kind of redirecting him.
SnowAngel:	ahhh, redirecting him. that's a good way to put it.
zoegirl:	why do i have to be this way? it's like i'm stuck in my stupid head, thinking, "crap, did i shave? do i smell? are my breasts too small? is my butt too big?"
SnowAngel:	zoe, your butt is NOT too big. if your butt is too big, then the rest of us should jump over a cliff and be done with it.
zoegirl:	and even worse . . .
zoegirl:	never mind. i don't want to say.
SnowAngel:	SAY IT
zoegirl:	no, cuz then you'll *really* think i'm a prude!
SnowAngel:	u don't like to pee around him?
zoegirl:	angela! as if.
SnowAngel:	then what?
zoegirl:	it doesn't have to do with peeing noises, it has to do with . . . other noises.
SnowAngel:	other noises? like body noises, u mean? like slurps and squelches?

zoegirl: okay, please let's not put names on them. i'm totally turning bright red.

zoegirl: but yeah, *those noises*

zoegirl: i want to get over it, i really do. i want to let go and let whatever happens happen. but i can't!

SnowAngel: wait a minute. if ur worried about noises, then u guys must have gone pretty far . . .

zoegirl: below the shirt, below the underwear. *but just barely*

SnowAngel: his or yours?

zoegirl: uh, both?

SnowAngel: holy cats!

SnowAngel: zoe, u r not a prude, ok? in fact i'd say ur turning into a sex guru. shit, girl, ur gonna outpace us all!

      ☺

Sat, Jan 8, 3:33 PM E.S.T.

mad maddie: it is a mistake to wear low-riders if u have an ass the size of texas. i am not saying this to be mean, but because it is the truth.

zoegirl: oh great! i just asked angela straight out if i have a big butt, and she said no!

mad maddie: U? ur a size two, zoe.

mad maddie: the ass in question is margo pedersen's. she was working at java joe's when i went by for a latte, and she had to lean over to get the milk. nuff said.

zoegirl: oh

mad maddie: u gonna c doug tonight?

zoegirl: yeah, at work. and we'll probably do something afterward.

mad maddie: ooh-la-la. give him a kissy for me!

Sun, Jan 9, 12:50 PM E.S.T.

zoegirl: hey, angela. i have something i want to tell u, but i'm not sure i should, only i really want to because it's making me all smiley inside.

zoegirl: can i tell you, or will it secretly make you sad?

SnowAngel: what r u blithering about? does this have to do with doug?

zoegirl: yeah, and i can't tell maddie because she'd make fun of me. so can i tell you, or would you rather i not?

SnowAngel: OMG, DID U HAVE SEX??????

zoegirl: angela, shhhhh!

SnowAngel: what, u think everyone in cyberland can hear?

SnowAngel: SO DID U????

zoegirl: no! of course not!

SnowAngel: darn

SnowAngel: altho not really cuz i don't think i'm ready for that

zoegirl: *you're* not ready? what about *me*?

SnowAngel: not everything is about U, zoe

SnowAngel: do u remember saying that to me, back when u first started lying? now u know what it feels like!

zoegirl: why are you snapping at me? are you in a bad mood?

zoegirl: talking to you isn't as fun as i thought it was going to be.

SnowAngel: i'm sorry, i'm sorry *drops to knees and hugs friend's legs*

SnowAngel: PLEASE tell me. i'll stop being obnoxious, i promise.

zoegirl: well . . . now it doesn't even seem like a big deal anymore. only, it is.

zoegirl: doug wrote a poem for me—isn't that sweet?

SnowAngel: awww! can i read it?

zoegirl: yes, because he posted it on poetry.com, which means anyone can read it. i think that's so cool, because it means he's not hiding it or anything. he wants the whole world to know.

SnowAngel: shld i go to the site right now?

zoegirl: i can just paste it in. but later you should visit the site and see for yourself how official it looks.

zoegirl: here it is. it's called "Miraculous Thing."

Miraculous Thing

Today all of the news is good news.
This morning a robin
lands on my porch
and beeps her hip hop
until dark.
I can't help tapping my foot.
I take her by the wing
and we dance into flight.
It is you, Zoe,
lifting me higher and higher
into the starry night
that reminds me
of your eyes and the sparkling
touch of your skin.
I may never sleep again.

zoegirl: isn't it beautiful and wonderful and perfect??? or do i just think so because it's about me?

SnowAngel: it's different from the poem he read at the poetry slam last year, that's for sure. that 1 was about dirty underwear.

zoegirl: no one's ever written me a poem before.

SnowAngel: no one's written me one either.

SnowAngel: ur lucky, zo

zoegirl: i know. thanks for being so cool about it.

zoegirl: but when it comes to maddie, mum's the word!

mad maddie: hey, a-boogie. chumley the psycho kitty scratched the hell out of my leg, and now i have three long gashes on my thigh. they look really cool.

mad maddie: is that sick, that i like the look of pain?

SnowAngel: yes

mad maddie: tell me ur not the same, tho. like when u get a bruise, don't u feel tough?

SnowAngel: i've always secretly wanted a black eye, to tell the truth

mad maddie: YES! that's exactly what i mean!

SnowAngel: we r sick little freaks, aren't we?

mad maddie: never said we weren't

mad maddie: so wassup?

SnowAngel: nothing much. i txted zoe earlier—she's doing well.

mad maddie: oh yeah?

SnowAngel: in fact i shouldn't tell u this, but i'm going to anyway. 🙂

SnowAngel: doug wrote her a poem.

mad maddie: oh good lord

SnowAngel: it's called "miraculous thing."

mad maddie: "miraculous thing"? what, now zoe's a bona fide miracle?

SnowAngel: it's sweet. it really is. it's posted under his name on poetry.com if u wanna check it out.

mad maddie: heck yeah, i'm gonna pull it up right now.

SnowAngel: did u find it? is it there?

mad maddie: "i take her by the wing and we dance into flight"??? we're not the freaks—he is!

SnowAngel: *chortle chortle*

SnowAngel: i take it that chive hasn't written U any love poems . . .

mad maddie: NO, thank god

SnowAngel:	doug must really like her a lot. *deflates a little, like a balloon* i'm embarrassed to say it, but it makes me the TINIEST bit jealous.
mad maddie:	**why??? cuz u wanna be compared to a robin?**
SnowAngel:	ha, i knew u'd make me feel better. 😊
SnowAngel:	seriously, tho, u can't tell zoe i told u.
mad maddie:	**excuse me, but it's on the world wide web. it's fair game.**
SnowAngel:	i know, but don't mention it anyway.
mad maddie:	**she should have told me. i hate it when she keeps secrets.**
mad maddie:	**but don't worry, i know how to keep my mouth shut!**

Mon, Jan 10, 8:35 PM E.S.T.

mad maddie:	**hey, zo. have u noticed mary kate's new way of talking? it's driving me up the wall.**
zoegirl:	what's she doing?
mad maddie:	**she, like, makes all her vowels long, like "agane" instead of "again." and she calls her mom "mum." i wanna vomit every time she opens her mouth.**
zoegirl:	i don't get it. is she trying to be British?
mad maddie:	**god only knows. it is nauseatingly pretentious.**
mad maddie:	**anywayz, that's all i've got. i'm off to meet chive at the awful waffle.**
zoegirl:	wait! that's it?
mad maddie:	**yeah, so?**
zoegirl:	nothing, it's just that we haven't talked in forever.
mad maddie:	**cuz u've been busy with doug**
zoegirl:	and *u've* been busy with chive, only you've told me hardly any details
mad maddie:	**whereas u, on the other hand, make it a point to tell me everything?**
zoegirl:	huh? what's that supposed to mean?

mad maddie: i've gtg, i'm supposed to be at the waffle house in 15 minutes.

zoegirl: then call me when u get back. or txt.

mad maddie: it'll probably be late, but fine. but you'll probably be asleep!

Mon, Jan 10, 11:39 PM E.S.T.

mad maddie: zo-ster! here i am txting u, just like i promised. u awake?

zoegirl: maddie, hi!

mad maddie: oh yeah? how high r u?

zoegirl: ???

zoegirl: so how'd the night go? did you have fun?

mad maddie: mmmm, waffles. i could eat five more right now. and chive played the jukebox and the jukebox played him. hehehehe.

zoegirl: what do u mean, the jukebox played him?

mad maddie: i mean what i say and i say what i mean.

mad maddie: aren't jukeboxes COOL, tho? i mean, it's like back in the good ol' days. a blast from the last.

zoegirl: i think you mean a blast from the *past*

mad maddie: oh man, do u ever feel like your teeth r too sharp? my teeth r really, really sharp.

zoegirl: what are you talking about? are you ok, maddie?

mad maddie: special lady! waitin on me at the waffle house. she's amazin! calling all those orders out. special lady!

zoegirl: omg, are you stoned?!

mad maddie: hey, i resemble that remark! hehehehehe

zoegirl: i'm serious. are you????

mad maddie: it's a song from the waffle house jukebox. am i chive's special lady? i wanna be chive's special lady.

mad maddie: and no, i'm not stoned. the word i could easily

	write to show u that i'm not would be trilogy. or in stone in frye in capsula. or i could go to bed even tho i know i'll be in big trouble.
zoegirl:	why r u gonna be in trouble?
mad maddie:	cuz the moms thought that too, ya know. about being stoned.
mad maddie:	oh man, i just realized something! u and the moms, ur like twins! u were separated at birth!
zoegirl:	maddie, i don't see the point in talking to you right now unless you're going to start acting normal.
mad maddie:	define normal. what's normal, zoe? r U normal?
zoegirl:	bye, mads. you're making me feel really sad.
mad maddie:	sad mad glad. how weird that they all rhyme.
mad maddie:	u should go eat a waffle! u can't be sad if u eat a waffle!!!

Tues, Jan 11, 10:34 AM E.S.T.

zoegirl:	angela, you awake? what time is it there, like 7:30 in the morning?
SnowAngel:	awake, yeah, but glendy's dad is gonna be here to pick me up any minute. what's up?
zoegirl:	angela, maddie texted me last night when she was stoned. it was *awful*
SnowAngel:	she was stoned? how could u tell?
zoegirl:	it was impossible not to. she kept going on about these random things and none of her sentences made sense and it was just scary. it's like she wasn't even herself.
SnowAngel:	yikes 😶
zoegirl:	i know. it's one thing to suspect that she's playing around with being a pothead, but it's another to see it in action. i didn't like it, angela.
SnowAngel:	did u tell her that?
zoegirl:	no, because there was no point. she was *stoned*

SnowAngel:	well, r u gonna tell her today?
zoegirl:	i saw her before homeroom, and i just played it cool. but she had to have known that something was up.
SnowAngel:	not necessarily. ppl see what they wanna see.
SnowAngel:	crap, mr. boss just pulled up in front of our apartment. TELL HER, ZOE! SHARING MEANS CARING!

💙

Wed, Jan 12, 8:44 PM E.S.T.

zoegirl:	hi, maddie. i have to tell you something.
mad maddie:	yeah, wazzup? did u catch mary kate's brit-speak today?
zoegirl:	it's not about mary kate. it's about u.
mad maddie:	meaning?
zoegirl:	meaning that i'm worried about you. it's been like this unspoken thing between us—even though i've noticed you feel quite comfortable telling *angela* about it—but i don't want to shove it under the rug anymore.
mad maddie:	shove what under the rug?
zoegirl:	think about it: with the whole doug thing, i didn't tell angela because i didn't want to upset her, and of course that just made everything worse.
zoegirl:	maybe friends *have* to upset each other once in a while. maybe that's what being a real friend means.
mad maddie:	is this about the other night? i was just messing with u, u know that.
zoegirl:	no, you weren't. u were . . . freaky, maddie.
zoegirl:	it scared me.
mad maddie:	oh please. ur such an old woman.
zoegirl:	i'm an old woman because i don't want you smoking pot?

zoegirl:	you weren't YOU, maddie. you could hardly string three words together.
mad maddie:	zoe, chill. THIS is why i never bring it up with u.
zoegirl:	no, you never bring it up with me because you don't want anyone pointing out that it's wrong!
mad maddie:	it's "wrong"? smoking pot is "wrong"? when did U get to be the morality police?
zoegirl:	it's wrong because it's bad for you—and you know it
mad maddie:	says who?
mad maddie:	u may not like the choices i make, but at least i'm LIVING. at least i won't look back at my life when i'm 100 years old and say, "i was too afraid to try that and i was too afraid to try that."
zoegirl:	because you won't have any brain cells left, that's why
mad maddie:	omg. maybe ur happy leading your boring safe life, but i'm not taking that route. i refuse to numb out.
zoegirl:	which is why you get stoned and drunk? because you don't want to numb yourself out?
mad maddie:	pot AMPLIFIES the experience, zoe
mad maddie:	forget it. u've never tried it, so how can u even talk?
zoegirl:	because i'm not stupid. because i like my brain in full working order, thank you very much. and because i'm not about to get high just to impress a guy who thinks life is one big party.
mad maddie:	god, ur self-righteous
zoegirl:	you don't have to get drunk or smoke pot in order to live life to the fullest, maddie.
mad maddie:	oh yeah? what DO u have to do? study really hard? be a good little girl and do everything everyone tells u to do?

zoegirl:	you're trying to make this about me, but it's not
mad maddie:	name one thing u've done recently that pushed u out of your comfort zone, that made your heart pound. and u can't say fooling around with doug, cuz that doesn't count.
mad maddie:	anywayz, u can't even give yourself fully over to that, can u? tell me that's not incredibly pathetic.
zoegirl:	i can't believe you said that
mad maddie:	are u saying it's not pathetic?
zoegirl:	well, it's not as pathetic as fooling around with someone else's boyfriend! it's not as pathetic as pretending that's the way you want it when really you wish he was yours!
mad maddie:	exsqueeze me?
zoegirl:	"i want to be chive's special lady." that's what you said when you were high.
mad maddie:	i did NOT
zoegirl:	those were your very words—go back and look! and i know that's why you're smoking so much, to make yourself stand out from whitney. but whitney's the one he's with, isn't she?
mad maddie:	so?
zoegirl:	so you're lying to yourself, maddie!
mad maddie:	whoa—i am so over this convo. u should hear yourself, man. u r majorly worked up.
zoegirl:	don't tell me i'm not living my life fully. don't tell me that i'm the one with the problem.
mad maddie:	"most men lead lives of quiet desperation." that's u in a nutshell.
zoegirl:	omg. show off for chive, not me.
zoegirl:	why are we even friends, maddie?
mad maddie:	WHAT?
zoegirl:	i'm serious. why are we even friends? i'm not trying to be mean—i'm honestly wondering. we

both get along great with angela, and when we're all three together, everything's fine. but we're not all three together. when it's just the two of us, everything seems to fall apart.

mad maddie: don't say that. that's not true.

zoegirl: i don't *not* want to be friends.

zoegirl: but it's like everything gets blown up between us. everything gets rubbed the wrong way.

mad maddie: not always. not even usually.

zoegirl: lots, though

mad maddie: i just think that if ur gonna point all this blame at me, then u have to look at yourself too. ur not perfect, zoe.

zoegirl: i never said i was

mad maddie: u sure act like it sometimes

Thu, Jan 13, 10:35 PM E.S.T.

mad maddie: hey, a. did u hear about zoe's and my big blowout? i'm sure u did.

SnowAngel: yeah, zoe called this afternoon. i'm so sorry!

mad maddie: she drives me up the wall. u should have heard how self-righteous she was being.

SnowAngel: well, like i said, i'm sorry.

SnowAngel: but . . . i kinda need to tell u that i don't entirely disagree with her. i mean, i've been worried about u too. *shies back to avoid wrath*

mad maddie: u don't need to be. god.

mad maddie: anywayz, the moms had already been riding me before zoe txted. i didn't tell zoe, but that's part of why i jumped all over her.

SnowAngel: riding u about what?

mad maddie: the same thing zoe was, my "alleged" poor decision-making skills. she was all, "ur not smoking marijuana, r u maddie?"

mad maddie: only she pronounced it mare-uh-joo-wah-nah. so lame.

SnowAngel: shit, maddie, does she KNOW?

mad maddie: she has her suspicions, which i neither confirmed nor denied.

mad maddie: actually, i denied the hell out of them. but where does the moms get the right to come down on me? she and dad are the worst role models ever. and has SHE smoked pot? yes, she has. last night she told me that she and the dads smoked "mare-uh-joo-wah-nah" at some party when i was a kid, and it almost cost her her marriage.

SnowAngel: whoa, your MOM smoked pot? your parents are so cool. why did it almost cost her her marriage?

mad maddie: she got all flirty with some other guy or something. it was like her little cautionary tale to scare me straight.

mad maddie: but the point is that the moms had laid all that on me—very serious and "this is your life, maddie"—and then zoe texted me and gave me the exact same lecture, only worse. can u see why i got upset?

SnowAngel: i guess

mad maddie: AND i somehow managed to lose my wallet at the waffle house, which is a major drag. i didn't have much cash in it, but it means i don't have my license. aaargh.

mad maddie: anywayz, i just wanted to explain the whole story. i don't want everyone hating me.

SnowAngel: nobody hates u, maddie. we could NEVER hate u.

mad maddie: u wanna know what's weird? and i could never ever tell zoe, so u better not either.

SnowAngel: what?

mad maddie: contrary to popular opinion, i don't actually LOVE getting stoned.

SnowAngel: i know, cuz it burns

mad maddie: yeah, there's that. but it also just kinda . . . makes things icky.

SnowAngel: like how?

mad maddie: it changes things. it's like everyone gets all distorted, and i can see what they're really thinking, and i don't like it. i can see how desperate we all are, cuz the layers get peeled off, and we're just these naked bundles of need.

SnowAngel: er, i'm not exactly following

mad maddie: like, ok, monday night at the waffle house? we're all crammed into this booth, and whenever brannen says something, he looks at me in this overly eager way. only i'm too busy looking at chive, who's too busy looking at whitney . . .

mad maddie: ugh. i guess i can't explain it.

SnowAngel: why do u do it, then? get stoned?

mad maddie: i dunno. cuz sometimes it's bad, but it can also be hilarious. like mad-laughing hilarity, where u just go on and on and on and u don't even know what set u off. that part's awesome.

SnowAngel: but we do that without pot, like when zoe was trying to learn how to drive stick shift and she kept rolling down the hill. remember? 😑

mad maddie: yeah, i know

SnowAngel: we USED to have mad-laughing hilarity, that is. we haven't for a long time.

mad maddie: i hear u

SnowAngel: tell me something funny. tell me something to make me laugh.

mad maddie: um . . . i can't think of anything

mad maddie:	wait, i know. today in english, mariah rath goes, "mr. phelps, it is SO cold in here. aren't u cold?" and mr. phelps goes, "noooo, i'm a little teacup."
SnowAngel:	???
mad maddie:	u know, from that song. "i'm a little teacup, short and stout. here is my handle, here is my spout."
SnowAngel:	it's teapot, not teacup
SnowAngel:	and that's not very funny
mad maddie:	it was at the time. mr. phelps is such a dork, u can't help but love him.
SnowAngel:	*blinks noncommitally*

SnowAngel:	zoe, why do ppl wear nude-colored hose? i am asking this as a serious question.
zoegirl:	um, because they think they look good?
SnowAngel:	but they don't. they never do.
SnowAngel:	glendy wore nude-colored hose today, with open-toed white leather sandals, no less. in january!!!
zoegirl:	ooo, that's bad
SnowAngel:	this morning she was all worked up about a bit of blueberry in her teeth that a guy she likes may or may not have seen, and i was like, "girl, u have bigger things to worry about."
zoegirl:	like nude-colored hose?
SnowAngel:	exactly
zoegirl:	poor thing
SnowAngel:	poor thing my foot!
SnowAngel:	she invited me to spend the night tomorrow night, can u believe it? i politely declined, and she goes, "oh, would tonight be better? cuz we can do it tonight, no problem." i told her i couldn't do that either, cuz mom wants me to get my room put together so that it doesn't look like i'm living in

a refugee camp. so glendy goes, "well, i'll come
help u. i know! i know! we can get matching
comforters!"

zoegirl: she did not

SnowAngel: she DID, zoe. and i've seen her comforter—it's this
crappy polyester deal with dolphins all over it.

zoegirl: so is she going to come help you decorate?

SnowAngel: r u kidding? glendy may have this illusion that we're
friends, but we're not. i already have my friends,
thank u very much.

SnowAngel: *droops* they're just not with me.

zoegirl: oh, angela. i wish i were there to help you
decorate.

SnowAngel: i don't wanna decorate. i don't even care about
decorating.

zoegirl: what did you say to glendy?

SnowAngel: i said, "thanks so much for offering, but how boring
that would be for u." and she said, "no, i want to,
really!" and i said, "that is SO sweet, but i'm not
roping anyone in to do my work." i just kept smiling
and not backing down no matter what she said.

zoegirl: ack. it kind of makes me feel sorry for her.

SnowAngel: don't u DARE feel sorry for her. she's snively.

SnowAngel: after she finally got it thru her skull that i wasn't
gonna invite her over, she got all pouty and said, "i
thought southern girls were supposed to be nice."
i looked at her like, "what drug r u on?" and she
quickly said, "just kidding."

zoegirl: hey now, southern girls ARE nice

SnowAngel: the point was, she needed to frickin take the hint

SnowAngel: that pouty crap might work with mr. boss, but not
with me. *wipes her hands of the annoying glendy*

zoegirl: you crack me up

SnowAngel: so have u smoothed things out with maddie yet?

zoegirl:	i don't know. kind of? she's just acting like everything's normal, only everything *isn't* normal, so it feels depressing and wrong.
SnowAngel:	believe me, i know all about depressing and wrong.
SnowAngel:	in fact, i'm gonna go stick my head in the toaster oven. bye!

Mon, Jan 17, 12:23 PM E.S.T.

mad maddie:	oh, martin luther king junior, i thank u for this day of rest. for without u, i would be in SPANISH right now instead of the lovely java joe's, sipping my delicious chai.
SnowAngel:	jealous. me want chai!
mad maddie:	here, i'll pour some thru the computer. gurgle, slurple, gack.
SnowAngel:	mmm, thanx. only now my keyboard's all sticky.
SnowAngel:	so zoe says ur being all fakey around her. r u?
mad maddie:	what?
mad maddie:	no, i'm not being fakey. how annoying that she would say that.
SnowAngel:	she says ur acting normal, but that things AREN'T normal.
mad maddie:	if things aren't normal, it's cuz of her. she thinks i'm too wild, but the reality is, she's too much of a wimp. she's like a timid little mouse. she's afraid to live in the real world.
SnowAngel:	ohhhh, i see
SnowAngel:	and it's your job to make her realize this?
mad maddie:	i never said that
mad maddie:	only . . . yeah! ur brilliant, angela. maybe it is!
SnowAngel:	maybe it is what? now i'm confused.
SnowAngel:	maddie?
SnowAngel:	come back! explain!!!

mad maddie:	hey, zo. wazzup?
zoegirl:	nothing much. you?
mad maddie:	nothin. i thought of u today in english, tho.
zoegirl:	why?
mad maddie:	cuz of something the little baptist girl said.
zoegirl:	what little baptist girl?
mad maddie:	she was talking really loudly to her friend with the mole, and out of her mouth came, "no way! shut the hell up!" it was very unexpected.
zoegirl:	are you talking about alicia arnold? you shouldn't call her the "little baptist girl."
mad maddie:	true, she's more of a big baptist girl, isn't she? anyway, the whole class heard and she turned bright red. and then she said, "it's your fault, mr. phelps. i picked it up from u, and now it's stuck in my brain!"
zoegirl:	mr. phelps says "shut the hell up"?
mad maddie:	in a jokey way. like, he'll look at us at the beginning of class and say, "all right, all right, shut the hell up. who's finished chapter 12 of 'Things Fall Apart'?" but now he says he'll quit on account of corrupting the big baptist girl.
zoegirl:	huh. weird.
zoegirl:	but why in the world did that make u think of me?
mad maddie:	cuz i started wondering, have U ever said "shut the hell up"? if alicia arnold can, then surely u can too. i give u permission.
zoegirl:	haha
mad maddie:	no, seriously. i think it would be good for you. ur so afraid of screwing up, but it IS ok to break a rule or two every once in a while. maybe if u did, u wouldn't be such a chickenshit.
zoegirl:	i'm a chickensh*t?

mad maddie:	um, yeah. just think about the whole angela/doug mess: if u weren't so wimpy, u would have told her in the first place. u said it yourself.
zoegirl:	u can't use that as an example. it's over and done with.
mad maddie:	but ur still a chickenshit—that's my point.
zoegirl:	i am not. stop saying that.
mad maddie:	then prove me wrong. pick anyone—anyone u want, as long as it's not me or angela—and tell them to shut the hell up. i dare u.
zoegirl:	that's the stupidest thing i've ever heard.
mad maddie:	why, cuz ur scared?
zoegirl:	no, because it's *stupid*
mad maddie:	that proves it—ur a chickenshit!

Tues, Jan 18, 6:55 PM E.S.T.

mad maddie:	hey, a. i totally called zoe on her bullshit! it was hilarious.
SnowAngel:	it was? what'd u do?
mad maddie:	i dared her to tell someone to shut the hell up. can u imagine those words ever coming out of zoe's mouth?
mad maddie:	i was like, "see! u criticize me for being willing to take risks, but isn't that better than being the perpetual good girl, locked in your land of repression?"
SnowAngel:	whatever, mads. u sound a little wacko to me.
mad maddie:	nah, i'm just gloating. u should have heard how defensive she got—hahahahaha!
SnowAngel:	u shouldn't gloat about your friends. u should love them. and when they're feeling defensive, or left out, or just lonely, then u should do whatever u can to make them feel better. u should only want what's best for them!

mad maddie: huh?

mad maddie: well, this IS what's best for her—to realize she's flawed just like the rest of us.

mad maddie: and now, off for a celebratory glass of nestle quik. l8rs!

Wed, Jan 19, 5:05 PM E.S.T.

zoegirl: ok, mads, i did it. are you happy?

mad maddie: u did what?

mad maddie: no u didn't. ur lying.

zoegirl: i'm not. i told chase dickinson to shut the hell up!

mad maddie: bullshit!

zoegirl: he was talking to kurt manheim in french about all kinds of disgusting stuff, that's what started it. he was all, "my rep's getting pathetic because i haven't had sex in over a month," and "that's why i need a girlfriend, someone older who can teach me stuff. someone who'll give me head."

mad maddie: he said all this in french?

zoegirl: not *in* french, as in parlez-vous francais. but right there in the middle of class, yeah. he sits behind me.

mad maddie: he's such a scuz. no way ANY girl would have sex with him.

zoegirl: so kurt said, "dude, you're crazy," as in, "people can hear you," but chase was all, "chill, nobody's listening." kurt said, "what about her?" meaning me. chase laughed and said, "zoe? she doesn't even know what 'giving head' means." then he poked me in the back and goes, "do you, zoe? do you know what 'giving head' means?"

mad maddie: what a dick

zoegirl: so i turned around and looked him dead in the eye and said, "shut the hell up, chase."

zoegirl:	i really really did it!!!!!
mad maddie:	whoa! nice work, zo!
zoegirl:	i know!!! 😊
mad maddie:	altho it's kinda pathetic that u see this as a big deal. any other girl would say that to him as a matter of course.
zoegirl:	i took your dare, simple as that. don't go downplaying it now.
mad maddie:	no, it's great. really.
zoegirl:	doug said so too. he was very proud of me.
mad maddie:	how r things going with ol' dougie?
zoegirl:	just fine, thanks very much. we went out for coffee after school, although actually we had mexican hot chocolate. have u ever tried?
mad maddie:	too cinnamony for me. in a bad way.
zoegirl:	i thought it was delicious. and doug and i had an awesome conversation, which was even better.
zoegirl:	i *really* like him maddie.
mad maddie:	didn't u already *really* like him?
zoegirl:	but now i like him even more. the physical stuff is still . . . a little tricky, but everything else is perfect. plus it's such a relief to like someone normal again, someone i'm allowed to like.
mad maddie:	as opposed to mr. h?
zoegirl:	as opposed to mr. h.
zoegirl:	i saw mr. h with cameron bryant today. it freaked me out. he was leaning close and smiling at her like he used to smile at me.
mad maddie:	u know what i heard from some senior? that every year mr. h has a "special" female student that he pays a lot of attention to.
mad maddie:	oops, i wasn't gonna tell you that—but now i did.
zoegirl:	oh
mad maddie:	sick, huh?

zoegirl:	yeah. sick.
mad maddie:	so u should be doubly glad u've got doug, that's all i'm saying.
zoegirl:	right, i am
mad maddie:	and that doug isn't pervy like mr. h
mad maddie:	or chase dickinson
zoegirl:	you know what else chase said? that he used to have this girl he "hung" with who gave him head for over an hour. is that possible?
mad maddie:	now that's just silly. blow jobs should not last over 30 minutes.
zoegirl:	ewww!
mad maddie:	ah, zoe, u still have a ways to go!

Thu, Jan 20, 4:04 PM P.S.T.

SnowAngel:	hey, zo. have u ever had wasabi cheese spread? it is sooooo good.
zoegirl:	isn't wasabi that super-spicy green stuff u get with sushi?
SnowAngel:	yeah, but this is a cheese spread with wasabi in it. it makes my mouth sting, but it's thoroughly addictive. *swipes last little bit up with cracker and smacks lips*
zoegirl:	mmm, you're making me hungry
zoegirl:	want to hear something sad? i saw mr. h hitting on cameron bryant—well, sitting really close to her in backwork—and maddie told me that cameron is his "special" student this year.
SnowAngel:	that's not sad. that's gross. he needs to go to a sex offenders' home.
zoegirl:	i know
zoegirl:	but the reason it's sad is because when maddie told me that, it made *me* feel sad.
SnowAngel:	WHY?

zoegirl:	i don't know
zoegirl:	because i wanted to be the only one?
SnowAngel:	zoe, no. u r soooooo much better off w/o him.
SnowAngel:	i take it u and maddie r talking again, tho?
zoegirl:	sort of, i guess
zoegirl:	huh. wonder how that happened?

Sat, Jan 22, 8:00 PM E.S.T.

mad maddie:	can't talk long—meeting chive for a night of wanton indulgence—but DUDE, am i brilliant. i have given zoe the best frickin dare ever.
SnowAngel:	dare? what do u mean, dare?
mad maddie:	it's just this thing we're doing. u gave me the idea, actually.
SnowAngel:	i did?
mad maddie:	i gave her the first one last week, and i just gave her the second. it's frickin genius.
SnowAngel:	what is it?
mad maddie:	can't tell. top secret. but it's going down tomorrow, on sunday, the day of our lord.
SnowAngel:	it's "going down"? what r u, a jewel thief?
mad maddie:	please. we're not stealing anything—in fact, the opposite.
mad maddie:	heh heh heh, it's so perfect to do it while he's at church.
SnowAngel:	do WHAT?
mad maddie:	g2g. byeas!

Sat, Jan 22, 5:07 PM P.S.T.

SnowAngel:	zoe, what r u and maddie up to? what's this "dare" business she's talking about?
SnowAngel:	zoe!
SnowAngel:	txt me!!!

zoegirl: oh man, angela. are you up?

SnowAngel: yes, but only cuz U NEVER TXTED ME LAST NIGHT and i'm dying to know what's going on!

zoegirl: omg, i haven't laughed like that in *forever*. at first i was like, "no, maddie, we can't!" but we did, and it was totally . . . purging.

SnowAngel: will u please explain????

zoegirl: we plastered bumper stickers all over mr. h's car while he was at church! we were very sneaky. we were like spies. and we stuck them on with super-glue so they'll be really really hard to get off!

SnowAngel: no way! what did they say?

zoegirl: one said "sticks and stones will break my bones, but whips and chains excite me," and another said "i'd rather be spanked."

zoegirl: also included were "ass pirate," "i heart llamas," and, my personal fave, "jesus loves you, but i'm his favorite."

SnowAngel: holy cats. he's gonna die.

zoegirl: he already did. maddie and i hid at the other end of the parking lot until church let out, and we watched him walk to his car. he was with some friends—including a woman!—and when he saw the bumper stickers, he about had a heart attack. the woman got a pissy look on her face, but his other friends cracked up. it was *supremely* satisfying.

SnowAngel: i'll bet

zoegirl: it was also supremely satisfying to see him try to peel them off. hahaha.

SnowAngel: right, hahaha. when did u guys decide to do this?

zoegirl: we didn't really *decide* anything. maddie dared me to do it, and so i did.

SnowAngel:	how come u didn't tell me?
zoegirl:	oh. well . . . i guess it didn't occur to us.
SnowAngel:	it didn't OCCUR to u?
zoegirl:	it wasn't that big a deal.
zoegirl:	wait a second, are you upset?
SnowAngel:	no, of course not. why would i be upset?
zoegirl:	if anything, i thought you'd be glad that maddie and i are doing stuff again.
SnowAngel:	i am, i am
zoegirl:	you want us to be happy, don't you?
SnowAngel:	i suppose
SnowAngel:	but maybe i don't want u to be DELIRIOUSLY happy, that's all.
zoegirl:	oh, angela
SnowAngel:	it IS pretty funny, tho. what u did.
zoegirl:	it would have been even better if you'd been with us—and i'm not just saying that!

Mon, Jan 24, 5:22 PM E.S.T.

mad maddie:	hellooooo, zoe. prepare to face your darkest fears, for i am about to issue the best and most thrilling dare yet. r u ready?
zoegirl:	what? no!
mad maddie:	well, get ready, cuz this is not a dare to be denied. it is the Dare of the Century.
zoegirl:	i hate to break it to you, but i think we should be done with dares.
mad maddie:	done with dares? surely u josh!
zoegirl:	i think we're making angela feel bad.
mad maddie:	ohhhhh, the old "we're making angela feel bad" ploy. sorry, charlie, but i'm not letting u off the hook that easily.
mad maddie:	r u ready to hear the dare?
zoegirl:	no

mad maddie: good, cuz first i need to give u some background information. imagine if u will a brightly lit classroom. it is 6th-period english, and all the students are filing in. but—what's this? instead of taking a seat, theresa ketchum scowls and drags her desk to the other side of the room. "theresa," mr. phelps says with a look of confusion, "why r u moving your desk?"

zoegirl: maddie, i'm serious—no more dares.

zoegirl: plus, i just realized something: why are *you* the only one giving dares? why don't i get to give *you* a dare?

mad maddie: and theresa says, "i'm moving my desk cuz i don't wanna stare at wendy's butt. her crack's peeking out of her jeans."

mad maddie: btw, didn't i point out long ago that low-riders r not for those who r substantially endowed in the buttock area? why yes, i believe i did.

zoegirl: i don't know where you're going with this, but i am not taking any more dares. and i am most definitely not taking any dares that have to do with butt cracks.

mad maddie: plz. but watching this little slice of life got me thinking: what stresses zoe out more than anything? and my brain answered, "BODIES. bodies stress zoe out more than anything."

zoegirl: what? that is so not true!

mad maddie: so what does zoe need to do? zoe needs to loosen up. yes, that's right, she needs to overcome her fears of being a woman, with all that being a woman involves. she needs—drumroll, please— to embrace her sexuality!

zoegirl: no no no no no

mad maddie: the other dares have been warm-ups. rehearsals,

	if u will. for it is this ultimate dare that will bring u to the peak of self-awareness.
zoegirl:	good grief, maddie. could u be a little less full of yourself?
mad maddie:	here is your dare: you are to glue two marshmallows to yr shirt—the OUTSIDE of your shirt—at approximate nipple location. then you are to stroll from one end of the mall to the other.
zoegirl:	*maddie*!
zoegirl:	you have lost it. i'm leaving now.
mad maddie:	"the great marshmallow-nipple dare," i call it.
mad maddie:	is it illegal? nooooo. is it dangerous? nooooo. will ppl stare at u? hmm, they very well might. i would, if i saw some chick prancing along with marshmallows glued to her nipples.
zoegirl:	no way i'm doing that, so just forget it.
mad maddie:	then ur a wimp, and u finally have to admit it.
zoegirl:	wait.
zoegirl:	i told chase dickinson to shut the hell up. i pasted lewd bumper stickers on mr. h's car. u can *not* tell me i'm a wimp!
mad maddie:	but this one's the real dare, the dare that's about U. and if u don't take it, then u have to admit that ur afraid to live your life fully.
zoegirl:	prancing around with marshmallows on your nipples does *not* constitute living your life fully!
mad maddie:	wimp
zoegirl:	this is so unfair! *no one* would do this dare!
mad maddie:	i would, and u know it.
mad maddie:	it's very simple if u think about it. u just have to get over your inhibitions, which is something u've needed to do for a long time.
zoegirl:	you're doing me a favor, that's what you're saying?

mad maddie:	tell ya what, they can be mini-marshmallows.
zoegirl:	gee, thanks
mad maddie:	so?
zoegirl:	noooooooooooooo!

mad maddie:	P.S. i googlewhacked "marshmallow nipple." four fucking million hits!!!
zoegirl:	maddie, you need therapy
mad maddie:	i'm just saying, that's A LOT of marshmallow nipples . . .
zoegirl:	once and for all, *no*!!!

Mon, Jan 24, 6:30 PM E.S.T.

zoegirl:	angela! where are you???? you told me to include you in things, but how can i if you're never there? i've been calling you for over an hour!
SnowAngel:	hi, zo! i just this second got home from school, which, btw, sucked. can i tell u something depressing?
zoegirl:	uh, sure
SnowAngel:	i was watching this girl during lunch, one of the many girls who have no idea i exist. she was sitting in the courtyard, talking to someone on her cell, and she was so animated. yip yip yip, like a little dog. and then she said good-bye and snapped shut her phone, and all of a sudden there was just . . . nothing. her face was blank, her body was blank, it was like she'd snapped herself shut along with her phone.
zoegirl:	yikes
SnowAngel:	and i thought, "that's me, that's totally me."
zoegirl:	i feel that way sometimes. like when i'm around other people, i put on this show of being interested and eager, and then when i'm

alone, i don't always know who i am. and i think how if someone were watching, like my dead grandfather or God or someone, all they'd see is this incredibly boring person.

SnowAngel: for me it's u guys who make me feel alive, u and maddie. without u, i'm just this floating blob of nothingness.

zoegirl: angela, ur not a floating blob of nothingness.

SnowAngel: seriously, i am!

SnowAngel: someone had on a shirt today that said, "if i seem to be getting smaller, it's because i'm walking away." that's me, zo. i'm getting smaller and smaller, only i don't WANNA be walking away.

zoegirl: oh, angela

SnowAngel: *recedes into smaller and smaller dot* *POOF!* *disappears*

zoegirl: you are never never never going to disappear

SnowAngel: what do u think my aunt sadie would do if i just showed up on her doorstep? she couldn't turn me away, could she?

zoegirl: um . . .

SnowAngel: aaargh, i don't mean to be so boring *gives self firm shake*

SnowAngel: so why all the calls? u said u needed to talk.

zoegirl: oh, right

zoegirl: er, it was stupid, actually. i'll bug you about it another time.

SnowAngel: u sure? cuz if ur sure, i think i'm gonna go take a nap.

zoegirl: try to feel better, ok?

SnowAngel: ttfn!

Tues, Jan 25, 9:59 AM E.S.T.

mad maddie: u gonna do it?

zoegirl: leave me alone, i'm supposed to be doing research.

mad maddie: maybe we should ask peaches what she thinks. why look, there she is at her desk. should i call her over?

zoegirl: leave peaches out of it!

mad maddie: at least i didn't say you had to do the great marshmallow-nipple dare at school, zoe.

mad maddie: think about it!!!

Tues, Jan 25, 2:07 PM E.S.T.

mad maddie: u gonna do it?

zoegirl: *no*!

Tues, Jan 25, 9:41 PM E.S.T.

mad maddie: u gonna do it?

zoegirl: go away!!!!!!!!!!!!!!!!

Wed, Jan 26, 3:35 PM E.S.T.

mad maddie: ur not gonna do it, r u? i mean, not that i care. i'm just saying.

zoegirl: oh, right, you don't care. that's why you've been buzzing in my ear like a fly for the last 5,000 years. if i had a swatter, i'd swat you flat.

mad maddie: i only care cuz i care about U. i don't want u going thru life like a scared little mealworm, that's all. isn't it better to be a fly than a mealworm?

zoegirl: what?

mad maddie: quiet desperation ... quiet desperation ... quiet desperation ...

zoegirl: fine. meet me at the mall in half an hour.

mad maddie: seriously?

zoegirl: but afterward, you belong to me. i'm going to give

you the worst possible dare, and you'll HAVE to do it!

mad maddie: **wh-hoo! i'll bring the marshmallows!!!**

Wed, Jan 26, 6:48 PM P.S.T.

SnowAngel: uh, maddie?

mad maddie: **hey, angela! man, what a day. wazzup?**

SnowAngel: i just got a really strange email from mary kate.
she hasn't been in touch at all since i moved, and
suddenly she emailed me this wacko message
about zoe. u don't know anything about this, do u?

mad maddie: **u got an email from mk? omg, this is great. what
did she say?**

SnowAngel: she said she saw zoe at the mall and that zoe had
MARSHMALLOWS GLUED TO HER NIPPLES! *bores
eyes into friend in extreme concern*

mad maddie: **it was awesome, angela. u should have been
there.**

SnowAngel: it's TRUE? oh my freakin god. zoe won't answer my
calls, and all i could think was, "maddie, maddie is
behind this."

SnowAngel: u made her glue marshmallows to her nipples?!!

mad maddie: **well, to her shirt, not her bare skin. and i didn't
MAKE her. it was a dare.**

SnowAngel: another one of your stupid dares? that's sick!

mad maddie: **don't think "sick," think . . . whimsical. playful.
a breath of fresh air.**

SnowAngel: i can't believe she actually did it. i can't believe it.

mad maddie: **imagine if u will: the mall is packed with irritable
shoppers, bored to tears with their predictable
lives. but hark! from the distance comes a hazy
apparition! it's . . . it's . . . it's zoe! she's charging
thru the crowd, nipples a-blazin'!**

SnowAngel: omfg

mad maddie: her face was bright red and she kept her eyes straight ahead, playing the "if i can't see u, then u can't see me" game. she was walking so fast that ppl had to dive out of her way. if it wasn't for the security guard, she'd have been home free.

SnowAngel: the security guard?!!

mad maddie: but now zoe can add "run-in with the law" to her resume too. i'm so proud of her.

SnowAngel: but is she ok?? she must be mortified!

mad maddie: if only she'd made it to Macy's. there was a group of nuns out front collecting money for the poor.

mad maddie: damn that pesky security guard!

SnowAngel: *shakes head in disbelief*

SnowAngel: u don't understand, maddie. zoe isn't equipped to handle something like this. if i was there, i would have stopped u!

mad maddie: but u weren't, were u? heh heh heh!

SnowAngel: u should be ashamed of yourself, madigan kinnick!

Wed, Jan 26, 7:20 PM P.S.T.

SnowAngel: i keep calling zo, but still no answer. i'm really worried.

mad maddie: oh pshaw

SnowAngel: so does she get to dare U to do something, now that u've publicly humiliated her?

mad maddie: yeah, i have to do whatever she tells me to do. i'm sure she's gonna make me quit smoking pot, but i don't care. i was gonna quit anywayz.

SnowAngel: really?

SnowAngel: i mean, good! serves u right!

Thu, Jan 27, 3:46 PM P.S.T.

SnowAngel: zoe, why haven't you answered your phone? r u too embarrassed to talk to anyone? even ME?

zoegirl:	huh?
zoegirl:	i guess my ringer's on mute. oops.
SnowAngel:	well, i just want to say how SORRY i am that maddie did that to u. i don't know what she was thinking. and i'm so sorry u felt like u couldn't tell me that day when u txted and said u wanted to talk, only i was so depressed that all we did was talk about ME. i'm so sorry i let u down!
zoegirl:	angela, hold on. you didn't let me down, okay?
SnowAngel:	ur nice to say that, but i know i did.
SnowAngel:	i called u a zillion times yesterday and never got u. what were u doing—hiding out under your covers?
zoegirl:	well, actually . . .
zoegirl:	i *was* under the covers, but they weren't mine, and i wasn't exactly hiding . . .
SnowAngel:	i don't get it. what do u mean they weren't
SnowAngel:	OMG, what r u saying???
zoegirl:	oh man, angela. it was nuts. the security guard at the mall lectured me for half an hour about "proper behavior for young ladies"—while maddie stood there smirking!—and after that, i was so embarrassed that i fled to my car and zoomed off. i just wanted out of there. but then about halfway home, i was filled with this incredible rush.
SnowAngel:	cuz it was over, u mean?
zoegirl:	no, cuz i *did* it!!! i actually did maddie's ridiculous dare. and having that knowledge inside me was like, WOW.
zoegirl:	it made me feel so liberated!
SnowAngel:	yes, but the covers . . .
SnowAngel:	just how liberated were u?
zoegirl:	liberated enough to drive straight to doug's house instead of going home. his mom wasn't there,

and we had the whole house to ourselves. and it was really, really great.

SnowAngel: *gulps* r u saying what i think ur saying?

zoegirl: no, angela, we didn't have sex. geez.

zoegirl: but we went further than we've ever gone before, and the best part is, i just let myself enjoy it. i was, like, on this adrenaline high, and i felt like i could do anything. so i just let go of all my zoe stupidness and went for it.

SnowAngel: oh

SnowAngel: here i was imagining u in the depths of depression. i felt so bad that i wasn't there for u, while all the time . . .

SnowAngel: u really DIDN'T need me, huh?

zoegirl: oh, angela. i *always* need you. don't u know that?

SnowAngel: i can't believe things worked out so well for u. i mean . . . whoa.

zoegirl: it *was* whoa. i never knew my body could feel like that. i know that sounds ridiculous.

SnowAngel: it doesn't sounds ridiculous. it sounds . . . u know. like a good thing.

zoegirl: i've always felt so bad at that stuff. like how i told you i could never get out of my brain?

SnowAngel: i remember. u wanted to be less inhibited.

zoegirl: yeah, like maddie. i've never admitted this to anyone, but i've always been kind of jealous of her, of how easy it is for her to give herself over to the moment. secretly, i've always wished i was like that.

zoegirl: not in a fool-around-with-every-guy-that-shows-up kind of way, but i didn't want to be frigid, either. isn't that an awful word? i hate that word.

SnowAngel: what, frigid? it doesn't sound like u need to worry about it anymore.

zoegirl: that's what makes me so happy! because i *did* let go of my inhibitions and i *did* lose myself in the moment! and not to get too graphic, but i was like, "ohhhh, so *this* is what all the fuss is about!"

zoegirl: i think doug enjoyed it too

SnowAngel: nooooo, u think?

zoegirl: all day long i've felt so strong inside, even when mary kate announced to our whole math class about the marshmallow-nipple thing. i just laughed like, "yeah? so?" and everyone looked at me like they couldn't believe it. like, "this is not the zoe we know."

SnowAngel: so yr saying yr GLAD maddie made that dare

zoegirl: no, i'm just saying . . . i'm not sure. that maybe it's not so bad to say "screw it" to the rules sometimes.

SnowAngel: oh *blinks in amazement*

zoegirl: wanna hear something awful, though? in my mad panic from the mall, i completely forgot about the marshmallows. so when i showed up at doug's, they were still there!

SnowAngel: oh no! what did he do?

zoegirl: let's just say that once i explained the whole crazy story, he took care of the problem. as in, the marshmallows are no more.

SnowAngel: uh huh. what a gentleman.

zoegirl: yeah, i love him

SnowAngel: for real? u "love" him love him?

zoegirl: omg, i didn't mean to say that. it just slipped out.

zoegirl: but . . . crap, angela. i think i do.

SnowAngel: *whistles* this is big

zoegirl: it *feels* big

zoegirl:	hey, thanks for listening. i'm sure it's boring to hear me go on and on.
SnowAngel:	um, no. boring is sitting alone in my room while everyone in my life moves on without me.
SnowAngel:	i'm happy for u, zoe, i truly am, but i swear i'm turning invisible.
zoegirl:	invisible? what do u mean?
SnowAngel:	last night at dinner i didn't say a single word. i didn't have anything to say, so i just sat there and ate my peas. no one even noticed.
zoegirl:	i'm sure they noticed. that's so unlike you not to be chattering away.
SnowAngel:	nope, cuz later i brought it up to my mom, and she was like, "oh, angie, u did so talk. of course u did."
zoegirl:	hmm. not the most reassuring response.
SnowAngel:	everybody else's lives r so exciting that they forget i even exist.
zoegirl:	angela, i am so sorry, but i've got to go. the doorbell just rang downstairs, and it's doug.
SnowAngel:	oh
zoegirl:	i'll call soon, promise!!!

Fri, Jan 28, 10:03 AM E.S.T.

mad maddie:	ah, we meet again in the lovely media center. so give me my stupid dare already, will ya? enough with the taunting looks, just get on with it.
zoegirl:	do u ever actually do your work when ur here? ever?
mad maddie:	i already know what it's gonna be, so don't think ur gonna pull one over on me.
zoegirl:	you know what it is, do you? then why don't you tell me?
mad maddie:	go on, just say it

zoegirl:	all right, then, here's your dare: tell chive how you really feel about him.
mad maddie:	**WHAT? that's not the dare ur supposed to give me!**
zoegirl:	that's the dare. are you a mealworm or are you a fly?
mad maddie:	**that's a stupid dare. that's the most stupid dare u could have possibly come up with.**
zoegirl:	oh yeah? then why is your face all red? i can see you, you know.
mad maddie:	**chive doesn't like me. he likes whitney.**
zoegirl:	then why does he kiss you? and why do you let him? and why are you packing up your books all of a sudden? has it gotten too hot in here for you?
zoegirl:	tell him how you feel. that's your dare!!!

Sat, Jan 29, 11:33 PM E.S.T.

zoegirl:	hey, angela. i know it's like two in the morning there, but . . . are you awake?
SnowAngel:	good god, zoe, i'm gonna have to strap a time-change clock to your forehead.
SnowAngel:	if it's 11:30 there, then it's 8:30 here, which means UR the one who's up late, at least for u. were u out with doug?
zoegirl:	yeah, we went out after work. but i'm not txting about doug for once. i'm txting to tell you what graham cracker said.
SnowAngel:	that 3-yr-old u think is so adorable?
zoegirl:	he fell and skinned his knee, and he got all worried when he saw that he was bleeding. it was just the tiniest bit, but he clamped his hand over it and said, "i am holding it in. i am holding it in." like if he didn't, it might all drain out.
SnowAngel:	poor little guy

zoegirl:	finally he let me put a band-aid on. he watched me really carefully, and then his eyes welled up and he said, "zoe, i miss my mommy." and i said, "i know. she'll be here soon." and he said, "i miss her because i love her. and when i love people, i want them with me always."
SnowAngel:	awww
zoegirl:	and it made my heart hurt, and i thought of you. ♥
zoegirl:	that's all.

Mon, Jan 31, 4:02 PM E.S.T.

mad maddie:	hey, zo. i'm at java joe's right now, and guess who i ran into?
zoegirl:	who?
mad maddie:	ian! with margo pedersen! AND THEY WERE HOLDING HANDS!
zoegirl:	ooo, maddie, ouch.
zoegirl:	you okay?
mad maddie:	am i ok? hell yeah i'm ok. it was a classic awkward moment, tho, the ex meeting the new flame. ian was like, "uh, maddie, this is, um, margo. she's, um . . . well, we were just . . ." and i was like, "dude, i know who margo is. we go to the same school. and ur allowed to date someone new, u know."
zoegirl:	weren't you upset?
mad maddie:	i did have the uncharitable thought of "she has a big ass, ha ha ha." but oddly enough i wasn't that upset. wanna know why?
zoegirl:	why?
mad maddie:	cuz i don't like ian anymore. i mean, as a human being, sure. but i'm not pining over him.
zoegirl:	ahhh
mad maddie:	he's not chive, that's the point.

zoegirl:	so you're admitting loud and clear in the light of day that YOU LIKE CHIVE. that's good, maddie. that's very good. now you just have to tell *him*.
mad maddie:	wait for it, wait for it
mad maddie:	i'm gonna tell him this weekend. we're gonna hang on saturday—i'll tell him then.
zoegirl:	for real?!
mad maddie:	i haven't done it YET. but i figure if u can glue marshmallows to your nipples . . .
zoegirl:	doug calls me "hot cocoa" now. warm and luscious with a delightful marshmallow topping.
mad maddie:	good god, one little dare and out comes your inner deviant. 😈
zoegirl:	ha ha ha. doug said the same thing, actually . . .
mad maddie:	doug shld send me flowers. he owes me BIG time.
mad maddie:	but for now, i'm outta here. i finished my chai and i've got some errands to run.
zoegirl:	like what?
mad maddie:	never u mind. it has to do with angela (and MAYBE u if ur nice), and it's a surprise. i just hate it that she's so depressed. it kills me.
zoegirl:	she left me a voicemail saying her mom's driving her into the city this afternoon. maybe that'll help.
mad maddie:	that reminds me, the other thing i need to do is swing by the DMV and apply for a new driver's license. every time i drive somewhere, i think, "shit, what if i get pulled over."
zoegirl:	why do u need a new license?
mad maddie:	cuz i lost mine, didn't i tell u? byeas!

Mon, Jan 31, 8:24 PM P.S.T.

SnowAngel:	maddie, my life has hit an all-time low. 😔
SnowAngel:	i know that hardly seems possible. how could i be lower than i already was? yet here i am.

mad maddie: but . . . i thought u went into the city today. i thought u loved the city!

SnowAngel: i do—it's the only good thing about being here. but guess who i saw while i was there? actually, don't bother, cuz u never will. i was buying a hot dog at the embarcadero, and the girl in front of me looked vaguely familiar. she turned around and it was JEANNIE STARR.

mad maddie: jeannie starr? she goes to northside, doesn't she? i think she's one grade above chive.

SnowAngel: yeah, she's a senior. that's why she was in san francisco, cuz she was visiting colleges. she says she wants to get as far away from home as possible.

SnowAngel: isn't that ironic? i was like, "here, u can have my life. wanna trade?"

mad maddie: that is so weird. i don't know that i'd even recognize her.

SnowAngel: it took us both a minute, cuz i barely know her and she barely knows me. but then she said, "wait a sec . . . aren't u angela silver? i thought u were dead!"

mad maddie: DEAD?

SnowAngel: she said, "i thought u died in a car wreck! that's what someone told me!"

SnowAngel: this is what my life has come to, maddie. i move away, and one month later everyone assumes i'm dead! 😳

mad maddie: that is so sad

SnowAngel: i said to jeannie, "what? no, i'm not dead." and she goes, "r u sure?"

mad maddie: good grief. she is 1 donut short of a dozen.

SnowAngel: i stuck out my arm and said, "u can pinch me if u want." and she did!!!

mad maddie: man. it's like that mark twain quote, "the reports of my death have been greatly exaggerated."

SnowAngel:	but the reports of my pathetic-ness have not. i might as well be dead.
mad maddie:	**DON'T EVEN SAY THAT. EVER!!!**
SnowAngel:	and then—THEN—i came home to find glendy's name on our caller ID 13 times. what cld anybody have to say that's that important?
mad maddie:	**how do u know it was the glendinizer? maybe it was mr. boss, calling for your dad.**
SnowAngel:	nuh uh, cuz she didn't leave a message, which mr. boss would have done. anyway, dad was at work, so if mr. boss needed him, he'd have just gone to his office.
mad maddie:	**did u call glendy back?**
SnowAngel:	no, i hit delete, delete, delete. *jabs button 13 times*
mad maddie:	**lord, angela**
SnowAngel:	and now i am going to take a very long, very hot bath and use up all of my mom's aromatherapy beads. and even that will not wash away the stain of my pathetic-ness.
SnowAngel:	i love u, maddie, but i hate my life!!!

Mon, Jan 31, 9:15 PM P.S.T.

SnowAngel:	glendy called AGAIN, and i finally gave in and answered. wanna know what was so desperately important?
mad maddie:	**do i?**
SnowAngel:	apparently she felt unloved. apparently she'd saved me a seat at lunch today and i failed to notice.
mad maddie:	**so?**
SnowAngel:	exactly! i was like, "and this was so important that u had to call me 13 frickin times???"
mad maddie:	**technically, 14**
SnowAngel:	all i could think was, "great. everyone thinks i'm DEAD except for u, and ur the 1 person in the world

i don't wanna hang out with. LEAVE ME ALONE, U
GROSS LEECHY PERSON!"

mad maddie: ha

mad maddie: what'd u tell her for real?

SnowAngel: seriously, maddie, i cldn't take it anymore, so i was
kinda mean. i said, "i'm sorry i didn't see u flagging
me down. clearly i am a worthless human being.
next time just don't bother, ok?"

mad maddie: ooo, way to tell it like it is

mad maddie: what did SHE say?

SnowAngel: first there was dead silence, and then she said
really coldly, "well, excuse me for trying to be nice.
excuse me for thinking u actually wanted a friend.
u pretend to be so sweet, but really ur just a
bitch!"

mad maddie: omg

mad maddie: angela, that was so uncalled-for. SHE'S the
bitch—u know that, right?

SnowAngel: it made me cry, maddie, isn't that ridiculous?
after she hung up on me, i just sat on my bed and
bawled.

mad maddie: oh, sweetie

mad maddie: if i were there, i'd spray paint bad words on her
locker for u. i'd take away all her Care Bears!

SnowAngel: *sniffles*

mad maddie: just think of it this way: maybe u've gotten rid of
the glendinizer once and for all.

SnowAngel: god, let's hope

SnowAngel: i'm going to call zoe and tell her about this
stupidness, and then i'm going to bed.

SnowAngel: thanks for listening, mads. night!!!

Tues, Feb 1, 6:33 PM E.S.T.

zoegirl: hey, are you home from school???? because it's

3:3o in california, if i finally got the time change right.

SnowAngel: i'm home, yup. wassup?

zoegirl: i want to ask your advice about something—
but first you have to update me on the glendy situation. how was she when you saw her today???

SnowAngel: *makes guttural frankenstein noise*

zoegirl: not so good, huh?

SnowAngel: actually, it was fine. u know the drill: wounded cold shoulder and poisonous glares. but at least i have her off my back, right?

zoegirl: *absolutely*

zoegirl: i'm still sorry that happened, tho

SnowAngel: oh who cares. it's just like everything else in my life, a big pile of poo. 💩

SnowAngel: what's going on with u? what do u need my advice on?

zoegirl: well, my mom and dad are going to this big law firm shindig on saturday night. it's called the prom, isn't that dorky?

SnowAngel: your mom and dad r going to the prom?

zoegirl: it's really just a fancy party, with a seated dinner and a live band. but it's black-tie, so everyone gets all dressed up. one of the partners at mom's firm decided to call it the prom as a joke.

SnowAngel: oh those crazy grown-ups! 😎

zoegirl: but what this means is that i'll have the house to myself.

zoegirl: eeek! i'm so excited!

SnowAngel: aha. r u gonna invite doug over?

zoegirl: i want to cook him a really nice dinner, wouldn't that be fun? and then . . . who knows where the evening will lead?

SnowAngel: hold on now. ur not thinking . . . i mean, are you
finally planning to . . .?

zoegirl: no! you always ask that, and the answer is always
no. the answer will *always* be no, okay?

zoegirl: but there's a lot you can do leading up to that . . .

SnowAngel: an empty house, a romantic dinner, a soft, inviting
bed . . .

zoegirl: so my question is, where should i go to get some
sexy lingerie?

SnowAngel: zoe! *jaw drops on floor*

zoegirl: what? that's allowed, isn't it?

SnowAngel: of course it's allowed! i'm just flabbergasted. who'd
have thought that u, of all ppl, would be marching
off to buy sexy lingerie? and for doug!!!

zoegirl: where should i go? victoria's secret?

SnowAngel: sure, that would work. what r u gonna get?

zoegirl: that's what you need to tell me. what *should* i
get?

SnowAngel: hmmm *taps finger on chin*

SnowAngel: is this something u plan to model for him, or will it just
be the delightful surprise beneath your clothes?

zoegirl: i'm not gonna model it for him! no, no, no. just
something nice for when we . . . u know.

SnowAngel: then i'd say it's time to go for the thong, zoe. god
knows ur the only girl on the planet who doesn't
own one.

zoegirl: a thong? i am not a fan of thongs and you know it.

zoegirl: anyway, don't u have to have a really good butt to
wear a thong?

SnowAngel: u DO have a really good butt. here's the criteria for
a thong: firm butt (preferably tan), no dimples, no
unruly hairs. do u meet the requirements?

zoegirl: ew, angela. does anyone really have hair on her
butt?

SnowAngel:	well, not sprouting from the cheeks or anything. i'm talking about from within the crevice.
zoegirl:	angela! sick!
SnowAngel:	so, good. u don't have butt hair—u can cross that off the list. now, for the firmness element. *cups hands in air as if squeezing* i don't think u have any problem there.
zoegirl:	oh my gosh, i am getting so nervous just talking about this.
zoegirl:	but okay, a thong. *maybe*. what about on top?
SnowAngel:	just get a good push-up bra with a little lace or ribbon on it. u'll be able to find one to match the thong, and if u can't, just ask one of the sales ladies to help u.
zoegirl:	no way, too embarrassing
zoegirl:	aye-yai-yai—i wish u were here to go with me!
SnowAngel:	yeah, me too *crumples into sad sack of a person*
zoegirl:	oh no, have i made u sad?
SnowAngel:	no sadder than i already was
SnowAngel:	i'll be with u in spirit. now go shop, u love-crazed fool!

Tues, Feb 1, 8:11 PM P.S.T.

SnowAngel:	hi, maddie. i am feeling very worthless.
mad maddie:	why?
SnowAngel:	cuz zoe txted earlier to ask for fashion advice, and it made me so aware of how pointless my life has become. she has doug, u have chive—and more than that, u both have each other. but what do i have? a big fat nothing. i don't even have glendy now that she's stopped talking to me!
mad maddie:	but glendy not talking to u—that's a good thing, remember?
mad maddie:	anyway, i don't "have" chive. not even close.

SnowAngel:	except ur gonna confess your love to him on saturday, zoe told me. and then he's gonna throw himself in your arms and ur gonna waltz off in a spasm of happiness.
SnowAngel:	i, probably, will be at home staring at my toenails.
mad maddie:	**that's bullshit**
mad maddie:	**do u really think he's gonna throw himself in my arms?**
SnowAngel:	so to commemorate my sadness, i've shaved off all my hair. i just wanted to let u know.
mad maddie:	**WHAT? u've been trying so long to grow it out!**
SnowAngel:	yeah, but what's the point? i don't have anyone to look good for, so i shaved it all off. i can be daring too, u know.
mad maddie:	**skype me then. prove it.**
SnowAngel:	um, my skype machine is broken
mad maddie:	**yr "skype machine"? uh huh. is snapchat broken too?**
SnowAngel:	ok, let me clarify. i *cld* have shaved it all off. i THOUGHT about shaving it all off.
mad maddie:	**your hair is so pretty. don't shave it off.**
SnowAngel:	i'm just so depressed. i have to do something.
SnowAngel:	my mom says i can go to atlanta over spring break, but that's not good enough. that's so far away!
mad maddie:	**ur coming to atlanta over spring break? angela, that's awesome!**
SnowAngel:	yeah . . . but i wanna be there now!
mad maddie:	**when's your spring break?**
SnowAngel:	march 21–25
mad maddie:	**that seems like a long way off, but c'mon. this is very very very good news.**
SnowAngel:	then why doesn't it feel like it? 😞
mad maddie:	**hold on, girl. u'll be here before u know it!**

SnowAngel: still sad. so sad i've started cutting myself, just fyi.

mad maddie: **so sad what a bad liar u r.**

mad maddie: **u can't stand the sound of your pulse, but i'm supposed to believe u could slice your skin and watch your blood ooze out?**

SnowAngel: ugh 😖

SnowAngel: u should go into counseling, maddie

mad maddie: **what? i'm not the one with the problem here!**

SnowAngel: i don't mean as a patient. i mean as a counselor. i can just see u talking to some poor distraught girl—much like ME, i might add—and saying, "u cut yourself, do u? u slice your skin and watch the blood ooze out?" u'd cure her in no time.

mad maddie: **good. does that mean i cured u?**

SnowAngel: maybe i'll start slow and build up. this girl in my math class uses a pink eraser to rub raw spots on the inside of her arm. i could manage that, i bet.

mad maddie: **please don't hurt yourself, angela. even in jest. and i think we shld have a moment of silence to send good thoughts toward any real cutters out there, cuz i'm suddenly feeling bad for making a joke out of it.**

SnowAngel: *groans* *puts head in hands*

SnowAngel: yr right, of course. kk, moment of silence, then:

SnowAngel: 😇 😇 😇 😇 😇

SnowAngel: r we done? r we good?

mad maddie: 👍

SnowAngel: subject change: did zoe ever make it to victoria's secret?

mad maddie: **ooo, baby. she just popped by to show me her purchases, and they're sexcellent.** 😍

mad maddie: **she didn't model them for me, for which i say a prayer of thanks, but she done made me proud.**

the bra is lacy and has a rosebud in the center, and she bought a thong to go with it. i am extremely impressed.

SnowAngel: she bought a thong? for reals? what's it look like?

mad maddie: er, like a thong? it's lacy too, and it's got the same rosebud thing going on as the bra.

mad maddie: pelt-woman calls her jesus sandals "thongs," btw.

SnowAngel: can u imagine pelt-woman wearing a *thong* thong? a real thong?

mad maddie: i will now slide a steel door over my eyes to prevent that image from entering my brain. there r few things i can think of that wld be more horrifying.

SnowAngel: my mom says that the key to a successful marriage is wearing pretty underwear. u might let pelt-woman know.

mad maddie: your mom says strange things.

SnowAngel: if u think she's bad, u should try my aunt sadie. i called her last night and said, "please can't i come live with u? please please please please please?" and she was like, "angie, i would love nothing more than for u to come live with me. we'd be two hip girls on our own. we'd have a blast! but hon, that's between u and your parents."

SnowAngel: then she told me she had to go cuz she was getting ready for a date, but before she hung up, she gave me a handy tip which i shld prolly pass on to zoe.

mad maddie: which was?

SnowAngel: to lean over when u put your bra on and really jiggle your boobs into place. "so many women have an extra inch of cleavage that remains under-utilized," she told me. "it's over by your armpits. u just have to shove it into place."

mad maddie: armpit cleavage. luverly!

SnowAngel: hi, mads! me again! 😊

mad maddie: couldn't get enough of me, is that it?

SnowAngel: i just wanted u to know how wrong u r about me, that's all. i may not be able to stand the sound of my pulse, but i'm quite fine with needles as it turns out.

mad maddie: so ur saying . . . what? u've taken up cross-stitch?

SnowAngel: i'm saying that i've pierced my nose. AND my nipple. i did it myself in my very own bathroom. just this second. *proudly thrusts out boob*

mad maddie: angela. cupcake. ur picking the wrong girl for your charade. u need to be telling this to zoe, not me.

mad maddie: anywayz, if ur going for shock value, u should tell her u pierced your labia.

SnowAngel: *eyes widen with appreciation* u r so right.

mad maddie: but don't say u did it yrself. that's too much of a stretch, even for zo.

SnowAngel: ah, yes. true true!

SnowAngel: zoe, i have something shocking to tell u, and i don't want u to get upset.

zoegirl: what happened? is something wrong?

SnowAngel: no, no, nothing wrong . . . other than everything, that is.

SnowAngel: it's just, well . . .

SnowAngel: i pierced my labia.

zoegirl: WHAT?

SnowAngel: i pierced my labia. i got this sudden urge, i don't even know why, so i walked into a body-art salon and just went for it.

zoegirl: omg. omg! did it hurt?

SnowAngel:	a little, yeah. well, ok, a lot. but i was very brave. in fact, the guy who did the piercing said i was the bravest of anyone he'd done.
zoegirl:	a *guy* did it? why, angela???
SnowAngel:	cuz he was the only person there. he does tattoos too. think i shld get a tattoo?
zoegirl:	angela, i don't know how to say this, but—and please don't be offended—is this a cry for help? sometimes people do really out-of-character things when they're unhappy. i mean, tattoos are fine, but do u honestly want to get one? you know how you are with needles.
zoegirl:	as for your . . . as for the other thing, if you took the ring or stud out right now, would the piercing close up?
SnowAngel:	oh, zoe. ur no fun.
SnowAngel:	no, i don't want a tattoo. and i don't want a pierced labia, either.
zoegirl:	you *were* just doing it for attention! poor angela!
zoegirl:	so go take the ring out RIGHT NOW! you've only had it for a day, right?
SnowAngel:	even less. i never got it done, zo.
zoegirl:	what do you mean, you never got it done? you just said
zoegirl:	oh. haha.
SnowAngel:	sorry
zoegirl:	did maddie put u up to this???
SnowAngel:	*blinks meekly*
zoegirl:	i should have known. what was i thinking? you can't even stand the sound of your own pulse.
SnowAngel:	must everyone go on and on about that? YES, i'm a blob. i admit it. you and maddie do these daring, exciting things, and what do i do? i plod thru school

with glendy trailing behind me like a cloud of doom. even when i go to the bathroom, there she is, glaring malevolently at me from over the top of the stall.

zoegirl: she does not stare at you from over the top of the stall.

zoegirl: does she?

zoegirl: anyway, what have i ever done that's daring and exciting?

SnowAngel: hmm, does parading thru the mall with marshmallow-nipples count? plus ur planning this fabulous night with doug, which requires its own kind of daring. and while ur cozying up with him, maddie's gonna be confessing her undying love to chive. that's braver than all the stupid-ass stunts she's pulled before.

zoegirl: well . . . ok, that's actually true. but you're brave too, angela.

SnowAngel: no, i'm not. if i was brave, i'd escape this stinking hellhole!

zoegirl: being in california isn't your fault, and being stalked by glendy isn't your fault either. just keep telling yourself, "spring break. spring break, spring break, spring break."

SnowAngel: u think it's that easy, but it's not. i can't talk about it anymore—it's only making things worse!

Thu, Feb 3, 6:02 PM E.S.T.

zoegirl: mads, you there?

mad maddie: i is, i is. wassup, girl?

zoegirl: well, i can't talk long because i'm heading out to dinner with my parents. i figure i should play the good-girl role while i can, so that they won't suspect anything about saturday night.

mad maddie: have u worked out the details with doug?

zoegirl:	my mom and dad leave for the prom at 7:00, so i'll start cooking then. i'm making chicken parmesan, steamed broccoli, and crescent rolls.
mad maddie:	**i thought for a romantic evening u were supposed to eat oysters.**
zoegirl:	yeah, like i know how to cook oysters. if i even liked oysters, which i don't. anyway, i told doug to show up at 8:00. i don't want him coming over until the food is in the oven.
mad maddie:	**what about kidding around? don't u guys usually work on saturday nights?**
zoegirl:	we traded shirts.
mad maddie:	**u traded SHIRTS?**
zoegirl:	oops
zoegirl:	*shifts. we traded shifts with other employees. this is our one opportunity to have the house to ourselves, and i intend to take advantage of every minute of it.
mad maddie:	**yeah, so that u can trade shirts, heh heh heh.**
zoegirl:	that was pretty freudian, huh?
zoegirl:	i'm *nervous*, maddie. isn't that silly?
mad maddie:	**it's cuz ur having impure thoughts. just think, after saturday u'll be a soiled dove.**
zoegirl:	a soiled . . . ?
zoegirl:	maddie, no. i told you already—we're not gonna have sex.
mad maddie:	**says who?**
zoegirl:	says me! *and* doug. we're not ready.
mad maddie:	**u say ur not ready, but what happens when the passion of the moment overtakes u? do u have a condom just in case?**
zoegirl:	oh, and where am i supposed to get a condom? you think i'm just going to march into the drugstore and

zoegirl:	*stop*! i am not having this conversation! doug and i are going to have a lovely romantic evening together, and maybe we'll fool around and maybe we won't.
mad maddie:	**believe me, you will**
zoegirl:	okay, we will. but we're *not* going to have sex.
zoegirl:	what about you? have you planned what you're going to say to chive?
mad maddie:	**ur joking, right?**
zoegirl:	if you're gonna confess your love to him, you need to know what you're gonna say. these things require thought.
mad maddie:	**cuz ur the expert now?**
mad maddie:	**zo, u know i'm not a plan-it-out kind of girl.**
zoegirl:	have you thought about it at all?
mad maddie:	**dude, i have sweat stains the size of buffaloes blooming from under my pits.**
zoegirl:	ick, maddie!
mad maddie:	**just imagine how bad i'll be by saturday when i actually see him. THIS is why i don't wanna think about it. i'll just . . . say whatever i happen to say. don't stress me out, ok?**
zoegirl:	fine, just as long as u don't wimp out. just remember: marshmallows!
mad maddie:	**grrrr**
zoegirl:	ack, my mom's yelling that it's time to go.
zoegirl:	but quickly, have u heard from angela today?
mad maddie:	**no. u?**
zoegirl:	she called from her cell a few hours ago. it was a little strange.
mad maddie:	**strange how?**
zoegirl:	because three minutes into our conversation, she said, "oh crap. here comes glendy."
mad maddie:	**i thought glendy was giving her the cold shoulder.**

zoegirl:	that's exactly what i said. and angela said, "i thought so too, but she's heading straight for me. and she's wearing a VEST."
mad maddie:	**i don't get it. what's the significance of a vest?**
zoegirl:	i don't know, that they're tacky?
zoegirl:	then in the background i heard this whiny voice, which i assume was glendy, saying, "angela? can we talk?"
zoegirl:	and then angela told me she had to go, but that she'd call me right back. and then she hung up.
mad maddie:	**huh. i wonder what happened.**
zoegirl:	and *i* wonder why she hasn't called me back.
zoegirl:	all right, bye for real!

Thu, Feb 3, 9:33 PM E.S.T.

zoegirl:	where in the world is angela? she still hasn't called or txted or anything!
mad maddie:	**give it a rest. she's FINE.**
zoegirl:	you don't think she's gone off and done something crazy, do you?
mad maddie:	**ANGELA? no, i don't think she's gone off and done something crazy.**
mad maddie:	**unless maybe it involves a daringly sparkly eyeshadow . . .**
zoegirl:	all right, all right. you don't have to make fun of me for worrying about my friend. sheesh!

Fri, Feb 4, 6:59 PM E.S.T.

zoegirl:	maddie, angela's phone is turned off, and i haven't seen her on FB or twitter or anywhere for two days. i called her parents' land line, and her mom says she's at *glendy's*!
mad maddie:	**at glendy's?**
mad maddie:	**that's unexpected**

zoegirl:	"unexpected"? that's all you can say?
mad maddie:	what do u want me to say?
zoegirl:	i want you to say that there's something very wrong with this picture, more than just "unexpected."
zoegirl:	she's disappeared off the face of the earth, and we're supposed to believe she's at *glendy's*?
mad maddie:	she hasn't disappeared off the face of the earth. sure, her phone's turned off, but she probably just spaced it. as for not being online, she prolly just hasn't been online when U'VE been online. did u think of that?
mad maddie:	unless . . .
zoegirl:	unless what?
mad maddie:	unless the glendinizer locked angela into the basement and forced her into a vest!!! ahhhhhhhhhhhh!
zoegirl:	shut up
mad maddie:	maybe she and glendy had to do a school project or something. try to find glendy's number and call her there.
zoegirl:	do u know her last name?
mad maddie:	sorry, charlie, ur on your own.

Fri, Feb 4, 11:59 PM M.S.T.

SnowAngel:	hi, zo. it's super-duper late, i know. so yr prolly not awake . . . huh?
SnowAngel:	yeah. (sigh.) figured.
SnowAngel:	i kinda need u, zo. like, i need to talk to u. can u tell i'm not so great at being all by myself at midnight with no one to talk to?
SnowAngel:	ok, well . . . i know i'm supposed to handle things on my own and all that, but i might not be that strong. i'll call u if i need u. mwah!

SnowAngel: maddie, are YOU awake?

SnowAngel: or are you snoring?

SnowAngel: *drums fingers on scratchy upholstery*

SnowAngel: yr snoring. fine. just don't call me unpredictable ever
               again!!!

Sat, Feb 5, 11:00 AM E.S.T.

zoegirl: maddie! i finally heard from angela, but it was
               weird. it was a late-night text, and it had to do
               with midnight and being alone and calling me if
               she needed me, only wanting to be strong enough
               not to have to. what was she talking about???

mad maddie: she txted me too. she made a cryptic comment
                  about not being unpredictable, maybe cuz for
                  once she was up past me??? does that count as
                  unpredictable?

mad maddie: oh, and she said something about upholstery,
                  which i didn't get.

zoegirl: well, i feel better knowing that at least she still
               exists. although her phone is still going straight
               to voicemail.

mad maddie: dude, she's fine. it's 8 in the morning california
                  time. she's prolly sleeping, which is what i wanna
                  do. power nap to rest up for my evening of sin
                  and debauchery.

zoegirl: tell me you're kidding. you're taking a nap at 11 am?

mad maddie: nighty-night!

Sat, Feb 5, 7:29 PM E.S.T.

zoegirl: sooooooo . . . ? are you at chive's?

mad maddie: not yet. we're not heading to his house until after
                  northside's basketball game, cuz whitney insisted
                  they attend.

mad maddie: are u cooking your fancy dinner?

zoegirl: everything's in the oven, and all i've got left to do is decide what to wear. what do u think: jeans and my peasant blouse or my black j.crew skirt and my gray cashmere sweater?

mad maddie: i thought u were gonna wear your fancy underwear.

zoegirl: but on top, dummy? i'm not going to open the door in my bra and thong!

mad maddie: well, don't ask me. ask angela.

zoegirl: don't u think i would if i could reach her???

zoegirl: so what should i wear??? doug's gonna be here in 20 minutes!

mad maddie: hmm. your peasant blouse is one of those off-the-shoulder dealies, right? i say wear that, for easy access.

zoegirl: easy access to what?

zoegirl: never mind. god, maddie, you and your smutty mind. i'm wearing the sweater.

mad maddie: u ask for my fashion advice and then do the exact opposite? what kind of friend r u?

zoegirl: a smart one!

Sat, Feb 5, 7:43 PM E.S.T.

zoegirl: oh yeah, i forgot to say one thing.

mad maddie: what?

zoegirl: don't wimp out!!!

Sat, Feb 5, 8:12 PM C.S.T.

SnowAngel: zo?

SnowAngel: remember how i said i'd call if i needed u? well, i need u.

SnowAngel: so call me

SnowAngel: soon, ok?

SnowAngel: call me soon, plz!

Sat, Feb 5, 8:14 PM C.S.T.

SnowAngel: maddie? u there?

mad maddie: angela! hello, hello!

**mad maddie: zoe's been worried sick cuz of not hearing from u,
btw. what's the dealio?**

SnowAngel: i ran away. i'm txting from a greyhound bus.

**mad maddie: hahaha. hence all the mystery? hence the veiled
reference to bad upholstery?**

mad maddie: where r u really?

SnowAngel: ???

SnowAngel: i really am on a greyhound. i'll be in atlanta in 12
hours.

**mad maddie: a-boogie, i already told u i'm the wrong girl for yr
games**

**mad maddie: and hey, sorry for bad timing, but text me later?
i luv u and can't wait to talk to u, but i'm kinda
in the middle of something. l8rs!**

SnowAngel: maddie, wait!

SnowAngel: MADDIE!!!!

Sun, Feb 6, 10:00 AM E.S.T.

zoegirl: crap, maddie

**mad maddie: u can say that again. 1 day—1 FRICKIN DAY—and
everything comes crashing down!**

zoegirl: i *knew* something was up. i just knew it! and
now i feel terrible, like i should have done
something to fix it all!

**mad maddie: what wld u have done? not even u cld have fixed
this one, zo.**

**mad maddie: wait a sec, how do u even know? oh god, my
mom didn't tell your parents, did she?**

zoegirl: your *mom* knows? how?!

mad maddie: oh let's see . . . cuz she's the one who had to pick me up from the police station?

zoegirl: the police station?! maddie, what are you talking about?

mad maddie: i'm talking about everything that happened with chive, and . . . wait. what r U talking about???

zoegirl: i'm talking about *angela*! she ran away from home and she's at the bus station this very second! only i can't go pick her up because i'm grounded, so you have to go. you have to go now!

mad maddie: she's at the bus station? the ATLANTA bus station?

zoegirl: yes. alone and hungry and . . . alone. go get her!

mad maddie: omg, she was telling the truth!

zoegirl: she didn't give me the whole story because her phone died, but apparently she just couldn't take it anymore. so she hopped on a bus and traveled for two and a half days to get here!

mad maddie: holy shit

zoegirl: yea, shit. but backing up a sec—the police station?!

mad maddie: i got busted buying pot, zoe.

zoegirl: oh my god

mad maddie: um, yeah, so i'm grounded too.

mad maddie: hold on—there is way too much going on here. angela's at the bus station, i can't go get her cuz i'm grounded, and u just said u can't go get her cuz yr grounded too. what r U grounded for?

zoegirl: my parents came home early from the prom. they walked in on me and doug.

mad maddie: oh no.

zoegirl: oh yes. it was AWFUL.

zoegirl: it was completely mortifying, and my mother saw way more of doug than she ever wanted, and i'm forbidden to leave the house until i'm 43.

mad maddie:	**fuck**
zoegirl:	yeah
mad maddie:	**and angela's waiting at the bus station.**
zoegirl:	yeah again
zoegirl:	what r we gonna do?
mad maddie:	**well, we have no choice, do we?**
zoegirl:	but how? i seriously cannot leave the house, maddie. my mom is livid. she would physically block me from the door.
mad maddie:	**lemme think**
mad maddie:	**ok, call the land line at my house got it? say you couldn't reach me on my cell. the moms will answer, and odds are she'll say i can't come to the phone cuz she'll want to punish me by keeping me from my friends. but that's good, cuz your job is to talk to her, not me.**
zoegirl:	talk to her about what?
mad maddie:	**about anything. use your good-girl charm and keep her chatting long enough for me to sneak out.**
zoegirl:	how do you know she won't see you?
mad maddie:	**cuz the phone's in the kitchen and my car's parked on the street out front. if all goes well, i'll be out and back without her even knowing.**
zoegirl:	if not, you'll be even more dead than you already are.
mad maddie:	**and so will you, cuz i guarantee that if all of this falls apart, my mom will call your mom pronto.**
zoegirl:	crap
mad maddie:	**yep**
zoegirl:	well, are you ready?
mad maddie:	**zoe, i was born ready.**

Sun, Feb 6, 11:23 AM E.S.T.

SnowAngel:	hi, zoe

zoegirl: angela. thank god. where are you???

SnowAngel: i had maddie drop me off at my aunt sadie's. aunt sadie is flipping out, btw. first she made me take a shower while she called my mom. then she made ME call my mom to reassure her that i really was alive.

zoegirl: what did your mom say? did she have any clue where u were this whole time?

SnowAngel: of course! *huffs indignantly* what kind of daughter do u think i am?

zoegirl: she *knew* you'd run off to atlanta?!

SnowAngel: well, noooo, i didn't tell her THAT part.

SnowAngel: what i told her was . . . well, it's confusing. lemme just walk u thru it.

SnowAngel: thursday i cut school early and bought my bus ticket, and after i did that, i called my mom and said i was spending the night at glendy's. (as if!) i told her we had an english project to do.

zoegirl: i *knew* you would have never gone to glendy's. that should have been my big warning sign. why didn't i listen?!

SnowAngel: and then friday, i called and said i was gonna stay for the whole weekend since we were having such a blast.

SnowAngel: that was a bit of irony in case u didn't notice.

zoegirl: when u weren't answering yr phone, i called yr mom, and she just sounded happy that u were off having fun. in my head i was like, "with *glendy*? i don't think so." but i didn't say anything.

SnowAngel: i'm glad—not that it would have mattered. by that point, there was nothing she could have done to stop me.

zoegirl: man, angela. i can't believe u hopped on a bus and came all the way across the country. i just can't believe it.

zoegirl:	weren't you scared?
SnowAngel:	i wasn't scared, exactly. it was more like everything felt . . . unreal. like there i was, trapped in my sucky life, and there was absolutely nothing i could do about it, right? but then i DID do something—and it turned out to be so much easier than i would have thought.
zoegirl:	actually, i kind of know what u mean. like after the marshmallow incident, when i decided to just say "screw it" to being the uptight me that i'd always been.
zoegirl:	although it is true that the uptight me would never have been caught naked in bed with my boyfriend . . .
SnowAngel:	poor zoe! i need more details on that, u know. my phone died right when u were getting to the good part!
zoegirl:	there is no way we're gonna talk about me when you just crossed the entire country—by yourself!— on a greyhound. my god, angela, what was it like?
SnowAngel:	like a really bad, really long field trip. mainly it was boring, especially in states where everything looked the same same same. instead of "wyoming," i called it "i'm moaning." "kansas" was "can't stand us," and "missouri" was "misery." that's what i did to pass the time, i made up new names for the states i went thru. i guess it helped keep my mind off what i was doing.
zoegirl:	nobody bugged u? nobody was like, "young girl on her own—better call the cops"?
SnowAngel:	not a soul. i was still invisible, apparently.
SnowAngel:	altho there was this one horrible man who boarded in St. Louis. he didn't do anything gross like try to molest me, but he was big and smelly and of all the

seats on the bus, he had to choose the one next to mine. his b.o. was REVOLTING, as in, i thought i was gonna barf.

zoegirl: ick

SnowAngel: so i got up and moved, with no excuses and no apologies. i was like, i'm not escaping california and the horrible glendy just to end up next to this bozo.

zoegirl: why *did* u escape the horrible glendy? i mean, i know why in general, but what happened that day when you and i were on the phone? i heard her in the background, and i heard her say that the two of you had to talk—did she say something specific that made you run away?

SnowAngel: *does air-blowing-out thing so that lips make p-b-b-b-b sound*

SnowAngel: i don't know if i can explain. mainly it's just that i was so unhappy already, with no end in sight. she just pushed me over the edge.

zoegirl: what did she say???

SnowAngel: she dragged me over to a private spot on the quad, looked at me very sternly, and said, "first of all, i'd like to apologize for all the things i've said to u in my head over the last few days."

zoegirl: no!

zoegirl: that's psycho, angela

SnowAngel: then she said, "but i forgive u, cuz i know ur having a hard transition. your dad told my dad all about it."

zoegirl: your dad discussed you with mr. boss?

SnowAngel: she went on and on about how she wasn't gonna let me push her away no matter how hard i tried, cuz she knew i was just acting out of pain. and then she put her hand on my knee and leaned so close that i could smell her breath, which smelled like taco salad. she said, "i know u miss your old friends from

	atlanta, but they're not here. i am. and i will never leave u, i promise."
zoegirl:	ewww!
SnowAngel:	and then the reality of that hit home, how glendy was gonna be there forever and ever, and how u guys were still gonna be in atlanta. and i was like, "no. i just can't."
SnowAngel:	so . . . i left.
zoegirl:	oh, angela. i don't blame you!
SnowAngel:	*puts hands on hips defiantly* and i'm glad i did, even tho i know it's gonna cause all kinds of problems. and even tho my REAL friends can't even come see me cuz ur both grounded, u idiots!
zoegirl:	omigosh, that's right! what in the world happened to maddie last night? did she tell you?
SnowAngel:	yeah, and it's bad. but i'm too tired to explain—text her yourself.
zoegirl:	what? NO! tell me!
SnowAngel:	whoa. woozy. all of a sudden i can hardly keep sitting up straight. guess that's what happens after being on a bus for 3 days, huh? ttyl!

Sun, Feb 6, 12:01 PM E.S.T.

zoegirl:	hey, mads. can u talk? i mean text?
mad maddie:	**well, no one's taken my phone yet, so yeah. u rocked with the moms, dude. she has no clue i was even gone.**
zoegirl:	that's because i stayed on the phone with her for an entire hour!!! i was like her therapist. she was all, "i don't understand why maddie would do something like this. you would never make such bad decisions, would you, zoe?" later she asked who else of our friends "participates" in smoking marijuana, as if i was gonna give her a list.

mad maddie: what a freak

zoegirl: no, she just loves you. but the worst part was sitting there going, "uh huh, uh huh. no, i'm sure maddie doesn't have a drug problem," when i didn't even know the whole story.

zoegirl: so while i'm very glad that you delivered angela to her aunt's, and i'm very very glad that angela herself is safe and sound, will you please tell me what happened to YOU last night?

mad maddie: u wanna hear the story of the Big Bust? fine, but it's not pretty.

zoegirl: spill

mad maddie: i met up with chive and whitney and brannen and meade after northside's basketball game, right? and brannen announced that he wanted some pot. so chive said, "ok, maddie and i will go buy it."

mad maddie: now before u get all judgmental, I WASN'T PLANNING ON SMOKING ANY. but i figured it would be a good chance to get chive alone, so that we could talk.

zoegirl: oh no. it's my fault—because of my dare!

mad maddie: no, zoe, it's not your fault.

mad maddie: actually, sure. let's make it your fault.

mad maddie: anywayz, brannen goes, "i'll come too," which was extremely annoying cuz i knew HE was saying it to be with ME. so then chive goes, "look, u two just go on. i'll stay here."

zoegirl: aargh!

mad maddie: yeah, but what was i supposed to say? so brannen and i took off to downtown atlanta, and at echo street i took a wrong turn, which meant that brannen ended up on the side where the sellers were, which actually turned out to be very lucky

	for me. so brannen bought a nickel bag, and off we drove.
zoegirl:	echo street? nickel bag? how do you know all this, maddie?
mad maddie:	do u wanna hear the story or not?
mad maddie:	five minutes later, i looked behind me and saw a police car. i didn't think anything of it, other than to remind myself AGAIN to get my damn license.
zoegirl:	i thought you already got your new license, that day you went on your secret errand.
mad maddie:	well . . . i kind of blew it off cuz the line was so long. nice move, huh?
zoegirl:	maddie. omg.
mad maddie:	uh huh, especially cuz it wasn't just a coincidence that the police were behind us. they turned on their lights and bleeped their siren, and i about crapped my pants.
mad maddie:	i pulled over, and the cops yanked me and brannen out of my car. they had us lean up against the door and they frisked us and put handcuffs on us. it was crazy. then one cop drove my car and the other cop drove me and brannen in the squad car, and we went to this big parking lot which was full of more cops and vans and other ppl who were obviously getting busted, just like we were.
zoegirl:	what are you saying, that it was a setup?
mad maddie:	the guy we bought the pot from turned out to be a cop named rudolph—no lie. rudolph took our names and asked which one of us had bought the "oatmeal," even tho they already knew it was brannen. then the other cop asked me for my license, which of course i didn't have.
zoegirl:	maddie! this is terrible!

mad maddie: they did a license check on a computer, and for some reason my license didn't come up—or maybe they just SAID it didn't. so the cop said to me, "why are you lying to us, girl? why are you lying?!" he was SO mean. and after a long hassle, they said that i could go, but that brannen was gonna get taken to jail. and then they told me that if i was caught out on the road again, then I'D be sent to jail.

zoegirl: can they really do that? send kids to jail?

mad maddie: guess so

zoegirl: but you didn't end up at jail. you ended up at the police station. i don't understand!

mad maddie: chill!

mad maddie: SO . . . i drove back to chive's and told everyone the story, and then chive and i took off to get brannen out of jail.

zoegirl: maddie, no!!!

mad maddie: but we had an unbelievably hard time trying to figure out where brannen was, and we drove around downtown atlanta for like two hours before finding the holding cell. turns out brannen's bail was $1,500, which meant that the bond would be $150. but we only had $98, cuz that's all we'd collected back at chive's. the bondsman we talked to told us that we needed to get the rest of the money and then come back with someone over 24 who had a responsible job. THEN he'd give us the bond.

zoegirl: good god, maddie. you know all this weird stuff that i would never in a million years dream of knowing.

mad maddie: believe me, i'd rather not. so we decided to drive to dunwoody and get my cousin donovan, only as

	we were walking back to my car we heard a man yell, "hey! you two! get over here!"
zoegirl:	oh no. what now?
mad maddie:	it was the exact same cops who had busted me and brannen after we bought the oatmeal from rudolph. i couldn't fucking believe it. they took us to the station and made us call our parents—and THAT'S why i'm grounded.
zoegirl:	ugh, what a mess. what an awful, awful mess.
mad maddie:	except there is one last thing. i did finish the dare.
zoegirl:	hold on. somehow in the middle of this, you found time to have your heart-to-heart with chive?
mad maddie:	we were sitting on this hard metal bench outside the police station, and i thought, "well, things sure as hell can't get any worse."
mad maddie:	actually, what i REALLY thought, cuz i'm an idiot, is that we were having, like, this big moment. we were going thru this really shitty thing, but at least we were going thru it together.
zoegirl:	so . . . what did u say?
mad maddie:	i told him that i liked him—more than just as a friend.
zoegirl:	and?
mad maddie:	it's not good.
mad maddie:	he put his head in his hands and said, "ahh, maddie." like he was in pain.
zoegirl:	uh oh
mad maddie:	he goes, "maddie . . . i'm with whitney." my heart was pounding really hard, but i made myself say, "why?" meaning, she doesn't get u. she can't keep up with u, she doesn't even get your jokes.
zoegirl:	but *you* do

mad maddie:	yeah, i do, and he KNOWS that, zoe. i could c it in his eyes. but he just shook his head really mournfully. he said, "i'm probably making a big mistake, huh?"
zoegirl:	like that's supposed to make it better? don't be man enough to actually *act* on it, just toss it out there like a consolation prize?
zoegirl:	he doesn't deserve you, maddie.
mad maddie:	then he took my hand and gave me one of his soulful looks and said, "we can still spend time together, tho. nothing has to change."
zoegirl:	is "spending time together" code for "fooling around"?
zoegirl:	i hope you told him to f*ck off!
mad maddie:	then my parents drove up, and that was that.
mad maddie:	the moms is totally bent out of shape. in fact i have to go, cuz she just knocked on my door and said in this pinched voice that she wants to talk to me. guess it's time for lecture #3 on The Evil of Drugs.
zoegirl:	maddie, i am so so so so sorry
mad maddie:	just another sucky day in suck land.
mad maddie:	u know what, tho?
zoegirl:	what?
mad maddie:	i am glad i told him, cuz now i know.

Sun, Feb 6, 7:33 PM E.S.T.

zoegirl:	hey there, sleepyhead. you awake?
SnowAngel:	hey, zo. my aunt told me u called a couple of times, but she didn't wanna wake me. sorry.
zoegirl:	that's ok, i just wanted to check in and see how you're doing.
SnowAngel:	about like this, i'd say.
zoegirl:	what's that, you with tire tracks across your face?

SnowAngel:	i just got off the phone with my mom. she said she's really upset with me for running away, but that she's also really upset that she didn't know how unhappy i was living in el cerrito. i was like, "mom, u didn't know cuz u didn't WANT to know."
zoegirl:	is she going to make u go back?
SnowAngel:	NO, cuz i refuse to. i told her that flat-out, and she said, "angela, ur our daughter. u'll do what we say." *rolls eyes*
zoegirl:	so what does that mean?
SnowAngel:	we're in negotiation. let's put it that way.
zoegirl:	what about school?
SnowAngel:	if i stay here with aunt sadie, i'll go back to school with u guys. but not tomorrow. not till everything gets settled one way or another.
zoegirl:	wow. i am so impressed with u, angela. i really am.
SnowAngel:	what about u—how's life on the home front?
zoegirl:	ehh . . .
zoegirl:	on the bright side, i didn't run away, and i didn't get busted buying pot. on the un-bright side, my mother saw my boyfriend's naked butt.
SnowAngel:	the dark side of the moon, like that pink floyd song. hee hee.
zoegirl:	i'm glad you can laugh about it
zoegirl:	it's just so ridiculous, my mom coming home from the prom and catching me and doug all over each other. and poor doug! he sent me an email saying he's never stepping foot in my house again.
SnowAngel:	and ur never stepping foot out of your house again, if your mom has anything to say about it. which will make things tricky, huh?
zoegirl:	well, i'll see doug at school, of course.

zoegirl:	you know what's weird? i'm not glad that mom walked in on us, obviously, but at the same time . . .
SnowAngel:	at the same time what?
zoegirl:	we stopped because my mom barged in on us. but if she hadn't . . . i don't know what would have happened. and that kind of scares me, because as you know, i wasn't planning on that.
SnowAngel:	whoa
zoegirl:	or maybe it wouldn't have happened anyway. it probably wouldn't have.
SnowAngel:	this time u really r talking about sex, right? about u and doug going all the way?
zoegirl:	we didn't even have condoms, angela. it would have been bad.
SnowAngel:	r u gonna buy some for next time?
zoegirl:	there's not going to *be* a next time for a very long time. i'm sure my mom's going to make it hard for me and doug to be alone together, even when i'm not grounded anymore. *if* i'm ever not grounded anymore.
SnowAngel:	and how do u feel about this? *raises eyebrows inquiringly*
zoegirl:	frustrated? relieved?
zoegirl:	i don't know!
zoegirl:	the whole night—until mom busted in—was amazing. and my body wanted more and more and more. but deep down i'm just not ready.
SnowAngel:	how does doug feel about it?
zoegirl:	he's like me—at least he says he is. although part of me thinks that if i said, "yes, let's go for it," he'd agree right away.
SnowAngel:	nooooo, really?
zoegirl:	i do love him, angela. it's just all so confusing.

SnowAngel: don't i know it. and not just boys, but EVERYTHING!

Sun, Feb 6, 10:01 PM E.S.T.

mad maddie: hey, u. u conked out?

SnowAngel: nah. i took a long nap. plus, my body's still on
                california time. it's only seven in el cerrito. isn't that
                weird?

mad maddie: do u wish u were back there?

SnowAngel: r u kidding??? not in the slightest.

SnowAngel: i'm sure i'll miss my mom and dad and chrissy
                eventually, but no, i don't wish i was there.

mad maddie: well, maybe i should take your place. think your
                parents would notice?

SnowAngel: madigan kinnick! *puts hands on hips* i came all this
                way to be with U. don't even tease me like that.

mad maddie: i just need a break from the moms, that's all. she
                can't get it into her head that my pot smoking
                days r over, that they were over even before the
                Big Bust.

mad maddie: the theme of tonight's lecture was that she thinks
                i have a "naive" philosophy toward life, which
                is that i have to try something out before i can
                make a decision about it. so she goes, "but u don't
                need to rob a bank to know that's bad, now do
                u? poison little children? put glass in halloween
                candy?"

SnowAngel: good grief

mad maddie: she also thinks that i was pressured into smoking,
                that chive made me do it. i told her, "why do u
                insist on believing that i can't possibly make a
                decision on my own? no one 'persuaded' me to
                do anything. it was not peer pressure!"

SnowAngel: huh. i'm not sure that's the angle i would have
                taken . . .

mad maddie:	the moms just shook her head and said, "i don't believe that, maddie. i simply don't believe that."
mad maddie:	aaargh
SnowAngel:	what about chive and brannen? have u heard from them?
mad maddie:	brannen's mom went down to the jail and got him. he's grounded, just like me, plus he has to do forty hours of community service. chive got off scot-free except for being yelled at by his mom. but i didn't talk to him long, cuz it made me feel too weird.
mad maddie:	i'm glad they go to n'side so i don't have to see either of them at school tomorrow.
SnowAngel:	as for me, i don't have to go to school at all. vacation day! vacation day!
mad maddie:	lucky dog
mad maddie:	will u do me a favor, then? i'd do it myself, but i can't, obviously.
SnowAngel:	what is it?
mad maddie:	i need u to go to 2620 moreland avenue. ask for a guy named willy.
SnowAngel:	excuse me? who's willy?
mad maddie:	tell him ur picking up the package for madigan kinnick. it's already paid for, so u don't have to worry.
SnowAngel:	maddie . . . what kind of errand r u sending me on? i thought u were done with your life of crime!
mad maddie:	oh plz. yeah, willy sells pot from behind the cash register, and i'm sending u to get it.
mad maddie:	give me a little credit, will ya?
SnowAngel:	what is it, then?
mad maddie:	don't open it until i tell u to. there's 1 for u, 1 for zoe, and 1 for me.
SnowAngel:	a surprise? 😄 i love surprises!

mad maddie:	so u'll do it?
SnowAngel:	of course. i have to go out anyway, cuz i need to buy a new charger for my phone. i kinda lost mine.
mad maddie:	well, thx. text me tomorrow after school lets out!

Mon, Feb 7, 4:05 PM E.S.T.

SnowAngel:	IMPORTANT MESSAGE TO YOU (MADDIE) AND ALSO TO YOU (ZOE) FROM ME (ANGELA)
mad maddie:	yes?
zoegirl:	hi!
SnowAngel:	i have picked up the "surprises" per your instructions, maddie. i have delivered 1 to zoe and 1 to u, which your mom should have given to u now that ur home from school. did she?
mad maddie:	i've got the box right here. u haven't opened yours yet, have u?
SnowAngel:	no, but i am extremely tempted!
SnowAngel:	i waited so that we can open them together. okey-dokey?
mad maddie:	let's do it, then. does everyone have her box?
SnowAngel:	👍
zoegirl:	yes!
mad maddie:	1, 2, 3 . . . open!
SnowAngel:	omg!!! *squeals and jumps up and down in a frenzy*
zoegirl:	maddie, it's beautiful!
mad maddie:	yeah, yeah, yeah. i know.
SnowAngel:	oh, mads, it's just like the one i lost!!!
SnowAngel:	are y'all's the same? do they both say "believe" too?
zoegirl:	mine does
mad maddie:	mine too. aren't i corny, getting us matching bracelets? i am so corny i can hardly believe it. ✋
SnowAngel:	i love it sooo much!
zoegirl:	me too, me too!

SnowAngel:	but i'm confused. my original bracelet didn't come from that store on moreland ave. it came from curiosities. and zoe, didn't u go back to curiosities after i moved? and they didn't have any more!
zoegirl:	that's true, they were all sold out.
mad maddie:	when u want something bad enough, u MAKE it happen.
SnowAngel:	but how???
mad maddie:	dude, i went to every single store in little five points, and NOBODY had any "believe" bracelets. finally this lady told me to talk to willy at a store called moon daughter, cuz he's a silversmith and he makes stuff like that. so i told willy what i wanted, i even drew him a little picture, and he said, "sure, i can do that."
SnowAngel:	aw, maddie, ur the best friend ever!
mad maddie:	no, u r!
SnowAngel:	no, U r!
zoegirl:	hey—what about ME?
SnowAngel:	*gives zoe a noogie* and u r 2, of course
SnowAngel:	we're ALL the best friends ever! *melts into a mush pile of affection*
mad maddie:	i put the order in for the bracelets a long time ago—back when u were still in california, angela. i wanted to cheer u up, and i hated that i couldn't do anything to make things better for u.
mad maddie:	but then u made things better for yourself. ur a stud, girl.
SnowAngel:	u know why, tho, right? cuz of u and zoe. if u guys were willing to take control of your lives, then i should be too.
mad maddie:	fat lot of good it did us. we're both grounded!
SnowAngel:	well, guess what? *giggles behind hand* i am too!
mad maddie:	wtf?

SnowAngel: i told zoe already, when i dropped off her bracelet.
               zoe, tell maddie.

zoegirl: she's grounded at her aunt's house, supposedly
               until the end of time. but we think her sentence
               will eventually be lifted. it's mainly just angela's
               parents' way of proving they can be long-distance
               parents.

mad maddie: long-distance parents?

mad maddie: what r u saying?

zoegirl: she can stay!!!

SnowAngel: i can stay!!! 😄 😄 😄

mad maddie: r u serious?

SnowAngel: i am the epitome of all seriousness. i have grown
               a beard, that's how serious i am. i will only wear
               tweed, with leather elbow-patches.

mad maddie: u r punch drunk

SnowAngel: *twirls about giddily* it's true, i am. i'm drunk on
               magnolia trees and sweet tea and true-blue friends
               forever and ever. 😊

mad maddie: i'm still trying to soak this in. yr parents said,
               "sure, u can live in atlanta"? just like that?

zoegirl: just for spring semester, and then they'll re-
               evaluate. if things don't work out, or if angela's
               aunt says there's a problem, then angela gets
               shipped back pronto. but that's not going to
               happen.

SnowAngel: especially not since i'll have u two to keep me
               straight. after all, ur SUCH good influences.

zoegirl: haha

mad maddie: maybe it's good that we're all locked in our
               respective houses, huh? at least it'll keep us out of
               trouble.

mad maddie: in fact, i dare say . . . yes, yes . . . this calls for a
               googlewhack!

SnowAngel:	what r u gonna try? "grounded girlies"?
zoegirl:	"punished pals"?
SnowAngel:	"caged cuties"?
mad maddie:	**ok, stop. ur starting to sound pornographic.**
mad maddie:	**i've got it, "virtuous rebels." cuz that's really what we r, right?**
SnowAngel:	and what's the verdict?
mad maddie:	**damn! 37,100 hits!**
mad maddie:	**will i ever find the one???**
zoegirl:	i found the one, and it's doug.
mad maddie:	**i meant "the one" googlewhack, fool. as in, the googlewhack that results in just one hit. must it all be about doug?**
zoegirl:	i'm sorry, i'm sorry. it's just that it's only been two days of being grounded, and already i miss him so much!
SnowAngel:	oh, poo. stop being so dramatic.
zoegirl:	me, dramatic? you're calling *me* dramatic?
mad maddie:	**quit yer whining. u'll see him saturday night at kidding around, won't u?**
zoegirl:	yes, only my mom has informed me that she'll be dropping me off and picking me up so that there's no "unsupervised contact." joy.
mad maddie:	**u want joy, try living at my house. the moms honestly and truly held up an egg this morning and said, "this is your brain." then she cracked it into the skillet. "this is your brain on drugs."**
SnowAngel:	mmm, scrambled eggs!
SnowAngel:	now that the weight of the world is off my shoulders, i'm starting to get my appetite back.
zoegirl:	doug did something cute at school, though. he gave me a hug, and without telling me, he slipped a bendy heart into my jacket pocket. it has little

	rubber arms and little rubber legs and a glued-on picture of his face.
SnowAngel:	awwww!
mad maddie:	**retch, retch**
zoegirl:	he wrote me another poem too. it's about how he values our friendship just as much, if not more, than all this other stuff. it ends like this:

> But for now just let me hold you close
> As I hear your breath and feel your sighs,
> And let me take a healthy dose
> Of your essence, smile, soul, and eyes.

SnowAngel:	that's so sweet!
zoegirl:	isn't it?
SnowAngel:	*jabs maddie in the shoulder* don't u have anything to add, mads?
mad maddie:	**er . . . what angela said**
zoegirl:	maddie! i *know* you're rolling your eyes, so you can just stop.
zoegirl:	but i don't even care, because i know there's something between us. he really is the one.
SnowAngel:	i think that's great, zoe
mad maddie:	**it IS great. i thought i had that with chive, but obviously i don't.**
SnowAngel:	*puts arm around maddie sympathetically*
zoegirl:	anyway, i've been thinking a lot about it . . . and my honest prediction is that we will, you know, make love.
SnowAngel:	*lets out low whistle*
zoegirl:	just not anytime soon, obviously
mad maddie:	**unless u do it in the supply closet at Kidding Around . . .**

zoegirl:	maddie!
mad maddie:	**jk**
mad maddie:	**i, on the other hand, will NOT be getting any action in the near future, cuz i called chive and told him that we're done fooling around. now there's a twist, huh?**
SnowAngel:	maddie! i am SO proud of u!
mad maddie:	**well, it's like my dad says. why buy the cow if u can have the milk for free?**
zoegirl:	yes, absolutely. and you'll *know* when it's real, mads, you really will. just like i do with doug.
mad maddie:	**yeah, shut up. that sounds a little too much like rubbing it in.**
zoegirl:	maddie, no! i'm not trying to rub it in at all!
mad maddie:	**whatevs**
mad maddie:	**but we've discussed it enough, ok? it's not easy, even tho i know it's the right thing to do.**
mad maddie:	**i always learn my fucking life lessons the hard way.**
SnowAngel:	ah, mads. but at least u've got us. 😄
mad maddie:	**so . . . u guys really like your bracelets? really and truly?**
SnowAngel:	i love mine. i completely and fully love it.
zoegirl:	me too. i can't wait to see what it looks like on.
mad maddie:	**OH! that reminds me. the rule is that we have to put them on for each other. none of this "bracelet breakthrough, i-don't-need-anyone-but-myself-so-i'll-tie-it-to-a-necklace" business, got it?**
zoegirl:	huh?
SnowAngel:	she's talking about this great method i invented of putting bracelets on.
SnowAngel:	but she's right. her way is better.
zoegirl:	that means we can't wear them until we're all together, though.

mad maddie: no worries, we'll find a way around this foolish grounding business.

SnowAngel: surely your parents will let u come see ME, won't they? dear pitiful me who's been gone for so long?

SnowAngel: my aunt sadie could be our chaperone and make sure that no one smokes pot or does the nasty. 😊

zoegirl: haha, very funny

SnowAngel: ahhh, my friends. i think things r looking up.

mad maddie: yeah, life is good, even when it sucks.

zoegirl: we'll see each other soon, then?

SnowAngel: very soon. so altho i'm signing off—*draws hand to heart emotionally*—it is with the comfort of knowing that it is the most temporary of farewells.

zoegirl: you make me laugh, angela. but yeah, i should go too.

mad maddie: laters, dudes

SnowAngel: and btw, i DO believe! i do, i do!

mad maddie: u sound like tinkerbell, u nut

SnowAngel: *wiggles cute little bottom suggestively*

SnowAngel: ttfn!!!

OMG, IT'S SENIOR YEAR!
TURN THE PAGE
FOR A SNEAK PEEK OF

l8r, g8r

THE THIRD BOOK IN THE
BESTSELLING
INTERNET GIRLS SERIES.

zoegirl:	maddie!!! i'm so excited, i can't sit still! i can't believe i'm going to see doug in 2 hrs!
mad maddie:	i hear ya—even i'm kinda excited to c the guy. i wonder if he's changed?
zoegirl:	do you *ever* check his instagram? he's gotten tanner. his hair is longer. he is even more handsome than he used to be, which seems impossible.
mad maddie:	deeper changes. like, changes on the inside.
zoegirl:	it's been SIX ENTIRE MONTHS. *6 months* of no doug!
zoegirl:	aye-yai-yai—what if he doesn't like me anymore?
mad maddie:	oh, please. doug is doug is doug, and no semester at sea is gonna change that.
mad maddie:	anywayz, haven't you guys been skyping every single day?
zoegirl:	that's true, but it's still different from being with someone in person.
zoegirl:	what i liked even more than skyping—maybe— were the snail mail letters he sent. well, snail mail postcards, mainly, from all the different places they docked. sooo romantic.
mad maddie:	speaking of romantic, what's doug gonna say when angela and i show up at the airport with you?
zoegirl:	er . . . hi, maddie? hi, angela?
mad maddie:	he's not gonna be pissed?
zoegirl:	why would he be pissed?
mad maddie:	that it's not just the 2 of you
zoegirl:	course not. 1st of all, his parents are going to be there. and 2nd of all, i'm way too nervous to go by myself.

zoegirl: i have to have my maddie and my angela—he knows that!

mad maddie: how's he gonna feel, waltzing back to school in the middle of our senior yr? is that gonna be weird for him?

zoegirl: PAST the middle of the year. i was *supposed* to have him back at the beginning of the semester.

mad maddie: i'm still reeling from the unfairness of that, btw. let's pretend i was the lucky 1 who jaunted off to Sea the World. would the administrators let ME take an extra month off to travel with my parents? i don't think so.

zoegirl: but you don't have straight As like doug—no offense.

mad maddie: none taken. i'm proud of my Bs. 👍

zoegirl: doug's mom called it "cultural enrichment." that's the excuse she gave the school. but i say he's seen enough of the world. now he needs to see ME!

mad maddie: ah yes, now it's time for him to be enriched in OTHER ways, nudge-nudge, wink-wink.

zoegirl: maddie!!!

zoegirl: i'm just glad we're going to be together again. i mean, he had a great time, and i'm proud of him for doing it, but he's definitely ready to be home.

mad maddie: god, and i am definitely ready to NOT.

mad maddie: seriously, if i could graduate tomorrow, i would. i'd be like, hasta la vista, baby! g-bye, atlanta— hello, santa cruz!

zoegirl: *if* you get in. which you will. i hate that you want to go so far away, though.

mad maddie: blame angela. if we hadn't gone to california with her over the summer . . .

zoegirl: too ironic. she escapes california to move back

to atlanta, and now all you wanna do is escape atlanta and move to california.

mad maddie: **U.C.S.C., here i come. go, banana slugs!**

zoegirl: is that honestly their mascot?

mad maddie: **it honestly is their mascot. it's 1 of the many cool things about them—their whole who-gives-a-damn attitude about typical college stuff like rah-rah football teams. that and the fact that they're 3,000 miles away, heh heh heh.**

zoegirl: oh, wow

zoegirl: maddie . . . i just realized something

mad maddie: **what?**

zoegirl: things really are changing, aren't they? we're seniors, we're going to graduate in 3 months, we're all going to go our separate ways . . .

mad maddie: **and this comes as a surprise?**

zoegirl: no . . . i just don't know if i'm ready

mad maddie: **i sure as hell am**

mad maddie: **repeat after me: change is good**

zoegirl: omg—no *way* did you just say that!

zoegirl: if angela were here, she'd be rolling on the ground.

mad maddie: **pardon me, but all i said was that change is good. why is that funny?**

zoegirl: oh, mads. aren't you the one who was outraged when they switched brands of soap in the girls' bathroom?

mad maddie: **the old kind was better! it smelled like lavender!**

zoegirl: and you have a fit if you can't start the day with your pop-tart and dr pepper. i thought you were going to stage a riot that day the drink machine was out!

mad maddie: **i'm a growing girl. i need my caffeine.**

zoegirl: and every time facebook changes its layout,

	you swear you're going to shut down yr fb page forever
mad maddie:	**your point?**
zoegirl:	my point is that you *hate* change
mad maddie:	**no i don't**
zoegirl:	yeah, you do
zoegirl:	it's cute
mad maddie:	**i thought we were talking about marching off into the big bad world, not what kind of soap comes out when you squirt the thingie in the bathroom. and all i was saying is that we can't stay in high school forever, even if we wanted to.**
zoegirl:	i know that. but it still feels huge.
mad maddie:	**anywayz, no reason to get worked up about it now. there'll be plenty of time for weeping and gnashing of the teeth before it's over.**
zoegirl:	i already gnash my teeth—that's why i wear a mouth guard at night. my dentist says it's the curse of being an overachiever.
mad maddie:	**an overachiever? YOU?**
zoegirl:	haha
zoegirl:	hey, can i tell you something stupid that's totally not worth dealing with, but at the same time i'm kind of disturbed by?
mad maddie:	**shoot**
zoegirl:	it has to do with jana. still wanna hear?
mad maddie:	**oh god. not THE J-WORD.**
zoegirl:	you and jana have a past. i'm just trying to be sensitive.
mad maddie:	**you might have to excuse me while i retch, but other than that, go ahead.**
zoegirl:	well, right before i left school today, i ran into terri. now, normally we wouldn't have even exchanged hellos, because of the fact she's

jana's best friend. but terri had been crying—her eyes were red and her face was all puffy—and i would have been a complete jerk to not say anything.

mad maddie: if i'd seen terri and she'd been crying, i wouldn't have said anything.

zoegirl: yes you would've

mad maddie: and if the situation were reversed, i wouldn't want HER to say anything, either.

zoegirl: well, i am a good human, so i said, "um . . . terri? you ok?" which made her burst into tears all over again.

mad maddie: c? that is why you should leave crying ppl alone.

zoegirl: she was *horrified* to be falling apart like that in front of me, i could tell. she kept saying, "i'm fine, i'm fine," but she obviously wasn't. so i took her to the girls' room and gave her a wet paper towel to press against her eyes, and we ended up sitting down below the sinks and talking.

mad maddie: so what was wrong? or rather, what terrible and awful thing had jana done to her?

zoegirl: they'd gotten into a yelling match over terri's hair, if you can believe it. you know how it's now the same shade as jana's? jana had cussed terri out for being a clone, and i guess she took it too far and said some really nasty things.

mad maddie: jana takes everything too far. she always has, but this year even more so.

mad maddie: she should go thru life armed with an apology and a complimentary bag of peanuts.

zoegirl: well, i felt bad for terri, even tho she's not my favorite person. i hate it when i fight with you or angela.

mad maddie: what r u talking about? we don't fight.

zoegirl:	so i said something like, "she shouldn't treat you that way," and terri said, "she treats *everybody* that way." i said she better stop or she won't have any friends left, and terri snorted. she was like, "poor little jana, alone in a corner. just her and her teddy bear."
mad maddie:	HA
zoegirl:	that's what *i* said. because it's such an oxymoron, the image of jana—mistress of death and destruction— clutching a teddy bear.
mad maddie:	ooo, nice use of the word "oxymoron." i KNEW i should have taken that SAT prep course.
zoegirl:	but terri goes, "for real, jana has this mangy old teddy bear that smells like spit. she takes it with her everywhere."
mad maddie:	???
mad maddie:	i've never seen jana with a teddy bear
zoegirl:	she leaves it in her car. that's what terri says. which is entirely possible. have you seen all the crap in the back of jana's station wagon?
mad maddie:	it's a mobile junk heap. it's disgusting.
zoegirl:	according to terri, jana's dad gave her the teddy bear when she was little, and she's unhealthily attached to it.
zoegirl:	its name is Boo Boo Bear.
mad maddie:	Boo Boo Bear???
mad maddie:	omfg, i am loving this so much. Boo Boo Bear!
zoegirl:	terri was like, "i can't believe i'm telling you— jana would *die*."
mad maddie:	heh heh heh, jana whitaker is unhealthily attached to Boo Boo Bear. suddenly the world is a MUCH brighter place!!!
zoegirl:	er . . . not necessarily. because 2 seconds later, jana herself stormed into the bathroom. "*there*

	you are," she says to terri, all fuming. "you're not even going to let me apologize?"
zoegirl:	then she noticed me, and her jaw dropped. she was like, "what are YOU doing here?"
mad maddie:	plz, it's a public bathroom. does she think it's her private office?
zoegirl:	my heart got all poundy, because—as you know—i'm a wimp, although jana had already switched to ignoring me. she said to terri, "get up, we're leaving."
mad maddie:	ok, that is the perfect example of the evilness of jana. she's bossy and she's mean.
zoegirl:	but amazingly, terri didn't obey. she said, "you can't treat me like dirt and then expect me to be your slave."
zoegirl:	"terri, get up," jana said, still very pointedly not looking at me. "we can talk about your 'issues' later."
mad maddie:	oh god
zoegirl:	so terri goes, "*my* issues? you're the one with issues! keep acting the way you're acting, and you won't have any friends left!"
mad maddie:	which is exactly what YOU said!
zoegirl:	i know! and for some reason that made me get all stupidly brave, and under my breath i said, "no one but Boo Boo Bear."
mad maddie:	holy shit! u da BOMB!
zoegirl:	i shouldn't have, though! it was totally unlike me!
mad maddie:	that's what's so great!
mad maddie:	did jana hear?
zoegirl:	she whipped her head toward me and was like, "WHAT did you say?" and terri goes, "she SAID, no one but Boo Boo Bear."
mad maddie:	gee, thx, terri

zoegirl: jana was speechless. i've never in my life seen her speechless, but for that single moment she was. big splotches of color bloomed on her cheeks. it was freaky.

mad maddie: cuz she IS a freak

zoegirl: then she pulled herself together and said to me, "you've got nerve, sticking your nose up. not all of us live in a perfect plastic bubble, you know."

mad maddie: exsqueeze me? what is that supposed to mean?!

zoegirl: she was trying to make me feel like a spoiled little baby, in comparison to her, the jaded and worldly jana.

mad maddie: who has a teddy bear.

zoegirl: her tone said 1 thing—see how cool and detached i am? i couldn't care less that you know about my stupid bear—but her eyes said something else entirely. she looked like she wanted to kill me. i'm not kidding.

mad maddie: well, duh. if anyone had to be there for that lovely moment, i'm sure you were the last person she'd pick. you or me or angela, that is.

zoegirl: that thought crossed my mind, but i tried to tell myself, "no, you're being silly."

mad maddie: except yr not. we have what jana doesn't have—actual true friends who lift each other up instead of tear each other down—and it's like a knife inside her heart.

mad maddie: think of it like this: jana's a dragon (SO not a stretch) and terri exposed her secret piece of weakness. so now jana's screwed twice: 1st cuz u know about Boo Boo Bear, and 2nd cuz u know how easily terri would betray her.

zoegirl: jana the dragon. i just hope she doesn't flame me.

mad maddie: if she does, she'll have ME to deal with.

mad maddie: now isn't it time to pick up your long-lost boyfriend? it's 5:15.

zoegirl: it is? EEEEEK! IT IS!!!!!

zoegirl: go pick up angela from her aunt's house and then swing by here. i'll be the 1 gnawing my fingernails to the quick!

mad maddie: i'm heading out the door. l8r, g8r!

Why were your books banned and do you personally believe that they should have been?

Lots of my books have teen girls in them. Teen girls sometimes talk about sex. Teen girls sometimes have sex. Lots of grown-ups would like to believe that this is not true. I am not one of those grown-ups, and I think it's important and meaningful to give readers stories that reflect reality—in a respectful way. Like, not salaciously, but with the intent of saying, "Let's look at how this story played out. How'd it seem to work out for so-and-so?" And then the readers—who are SMART, damn it—can grapple with those issues themselves. And no, I do not believe my books should have been banned. I do not believe that any author should be banned, ever. Freedom of speech, dude. :)

What's your response when you are censored? Are you ever frustrated, or do you take pride in it?

At first I cried. And called my editor and apologized, because I felt so terrible about it. Now I take pride . . . but it requires a bit of emotional effort, because it still hurts to have people say, out loud and with venom, "Your books suck. YOU suck."

What was your favorite part of writing the Internet Girls series?

My fave part of writing this series was NOT HAVING TO WRITE SETTING. I hate setting. In other books that aren't purely written in text/IMs, my annoying (awesome) editor makes me include setting, and it is hard.

Which of your characters is most like you, and which character do you wish you were more like?

I'm most like Winnie from the Winnie Years series. She's a good girl, funny, tries to do the right thing. Often gets into embarrassing situations. I once ran over a squirrel on my bike.

Whom do I wish I were more like? I'm going to go with Cat from *Shine*, because she has courage in spades. She doesn't let the haters get to her. Sometimes I do.

How do you come up with your characters?

I follow my children around as they go through their lives and I spy on them. I wear a trench coat and carry a notepad. I am vair vair subtle.

Except, really, I do.

As an author, what's your average day like?

Oh, an average day of writing means MAKING MYSELF WRITE. And then thinking, "Oh, this is fun." And then writing some more.

What do you think books offer that other forms of entertainment don't?

Books engage readers in a more intimate way than other forms of entertainment/media, I think. They encourage critical thinking.

What is your very best life advice?

Best advice? Sheesh. Imagine life is like this: You're waiting at a red light. You're stuck there. You didn't choose to be, but there you are. How are you going to spend your time? Bitching and moaning and looking at your watch, or thinking INTERESTING thoughts? Looking at the beautiful sky? Laughing at a joke? So, use this life WISELY—we're dead a lot longer than we're alive—and leave the universe a better place than when you got here.

ACKNOWLEDGMENTS

Oh, li'l dudes, I thank you:

Liz Baltich, Kelly Dean, Todd Mitchell, Laura Pritchett, and Jack Martin, for being the best readers a girl could ask for; Derek DeCoux, poet extraordinaire and all-around cool guy; my agent, Barry Goldblatt, for assuring me that I don't suck whenever I convince myself I do; the groovy folks at Abrams, for giving me such a wonderful book-y home; Erica Finkel, goddess of cool and slave driver of scary fierceness; and the inestimable Susan Van Metre, for making me write the damn novel again and again and AGAIN. *flings self on dagger and perishes*

Thanks to Al, who wanted Maddie to say "blah, blah, blah." (And Jamie and Mirabelle, thank you, too, just for being so cute.)

And finally, huge hugs and thanks to Maria Middleton for giving this baby its sparkly new updated look!

LAUREN MYRACLE is the author of many books for teens and young people, including the *New York Times* bestselling Internet Girls series, *Shine, Rhymes with Witches, Bliss, The Infinite Moment of Us,* and the Flower Power series. She lives with her family in Fort Collins, Colorado. Visit her online at laurenmyracle.com.